Acting in

New *X Rated* titles from *X Libris*:

Game of Masks	Roxanne Morgan
Who Dares Sins	Roxanne Morgan

The *X Libris* series:

The Pleasure Principle	Emma Allan
The Discipline of Pearls	Susan Swann
Arousing Anna	Nina Sheridan
Sleeping Partner	Mariah Greene
Playing the Game	Selina Seymour
Pleasuring Pamela	Nina Sheridan
The Women's Club	Vanessa Davies
Saturnalia	Zara Devereux
Velvet Touch	Zara Devereux
The Gambler	Tallulah Sharpe
Eternal Kiss	Anastasia Dubois
Forbidden Desires	Marina Anderson
Wild Silk	Zara Devereux
Letting Go	Cathy Hunter
Two Women	Emma Allan
Blue Notes	Stephanie Ash
Pleasure Bound	Susan Swann
Educating Eleanor	Nina Sheridan
Silken Bonds	Zara Devereux
Fast Learner	Ginnie Bond
Chrysalis	Natalie Blake
Rough Trade	Emma Allan
Liberating Lydia	Nine Sheridan
Cirque Erotique	Mikki Leone
Lessons in Lust	Emma Allan
Lottery Lovers	Vanessa Davies
Bets	Roxanne Morgan
Power Games	Alexa Caine
Isle of Desire	Zara Devereux
Overexposed	Ginnie Bond
Perfect Partners	Natalie Blake
Black Stockings	Emma Allan
Legacy of Desire	Marina Anderson

Acting It Out

Vanessa Davies

X RATED

An *X Libris* Book

First published in Great Britain in 1996
by Little, Brown and Company
This edition published in 1999

*All characters in this publication are
fictitious and any resemblance to real persons,
living or dead, is purely coincidental.*

A CIP catalogue record for this book
is available from the British Library.

ISBN 0 7515 2937 0

Typeset by Derek Doyle & Associates,
Mold, Clwyd, North Wales
Printed and bound in Great Britain by
Clays Ltd, St Ives plc

X Libris
A Division of
Little, Brown and Company (UK)
Brettenham House
Lancaster Place
London WC2E 7EN

Acting It Out

Chapter One

LYNNE SANDERS TOOK a deep breath followed by a long, hard look at herself in the mirror. She was startled to see someone that she only half recognised. The hazel eyes were undoubtedly her own, but her hair was now a subtle dark blonde, short and brushed forward in a windswept style that somehow changed her face to a heart shape. Beneath the wispy fringe her eyes looked larger – and greener, too. Her skin appeared flawless, with a warm glow, and her lips were a shade of pinkish bronze that she'd never have chosen for herself. She had to admit that both the hair stylist and the make-up artist had created a stunning new look for her.

'I don't quite know what to say,' Lynne admitted to Debbi, the editor of *Face and Figure* who'd run the competition. 'I'd never have believed I could look so . . . so . . .'

'Glamorous?' Debbi laughed. 'Wait till you see what Marianne has lined up for you! Let's get going shall we? We're running a bit behind schedule.'

The studios of Sphere TV were connected by a

maze of corridors. As Lynne followed Debbi her pulse was racing at the prospect of meeting the cast of *Night Owls*. That was the best part of the prize. She was an avid fan of the adult soap and tonight she'd be dining with one of the stars, Blake Harrison. Lynne had often fantasised about the handsome actor, but would he live up to her expectations when she spent a whole evening with him? It still didn't seem real, but perhaps by the time they'd finished transforming her appearance she would believe that such things could happen – to the new-look Lynne Sanders.

They reached 'wardrobe' where an ex-model called Marianne awaited them. Several outfits were hanging on a rail, mostly in colours and styles that Lynne would have shunned, but Carol assured her that they were perfect for her new colouring. 'Try the Luigi Varoni dress,' she advised.

Lynne was convinced she'd look terrible in it. At least she was wearing decent underwear. She'd treated herself to a set in white, lace-trimmed silk for the occasion.

As Marianne zipped her up before the long mirror Lynne hardly dared look. When she did, she let out an involuntary gasp. The dress was short, soft pink and had a cutaway over her chest revealing a hint of cleavage. Magically she'd been transformed into the sexy, sophisticated, fun-loving woman she had always secretly wanted to be. At least, that was the outward impression. But could she carry it off? More to the point, could she face Blake Harrison looking like that?

There were elegant high-heeled shoes, a black velvet jacket and matching bag to complete the outfit. Lynne paraded with growing enthusiasm, giving the editor a warm smile. 'I'm really pleased with my new look. Thank you very much, Debbi.'

'I'm so glad, but the best is yet to come. After Pete's taken a few photos, I'll pop you along to Studio B. You can watch some of the filming, then you'll meet Blake.'

Soon Lynne stood in the studio gallery watching the action below through the huge window. A girl called Kate was explaining what was going on. 'This scene's between Hugo and his new girlfriend, Monica. It's six episodes on from last Saturday's. Did you see it?'

'Oh yes! I watch it every weekend.'

'You'll know the storyline then. I can't give too much away, obviously, but you'll gather that Blake will be in trouble with Suzi when she finds out about Monica.'

Lynne looked down on the studio floor, where a bedroom scene was in progress. The actress playing Monica was lying under the duvet, and it was obvious that she was naked from the waist up. The tops of her rather large breasts reared provocatively above the duvet. Her expression, however, was one of impatient boredom.

Blake was wearing the bottom half of a pair of silk pyjamas and standing by the bed, talking to a man with earphones and a script. His tanned torso, covered with a film of sweat, was gleaming under the studio lights. Sexy, Lynne thought, feeling her pulse throb more insistently. His broad shoulders and muscled chest seemed out of place surrounded by cables and cameras, as did the bedroom set with its floral décor. Lynne reminded herself that it was all part of the illusion called television.

Suddenly the actor turned and playfully shook his

fist at the control room. The director and some of the others laughed. Blake, obviously deciding to play to the gallery, crossed his thighs coyly as he stood and toyed with the pyjama cord.

Kate giggled. 'Blake's been told to remove his pyjama bottoms. He thought he wouldn't have to. Mind you, I don't think Andrea will object.'

Lynne let the innuendo pass, not wishing to appear eager for gossip. She knew of Blake's media image as a womaniser, and even at a distance she could see how he'd obtained it. She watched fascinated as, with his back to the gallery, he slipped off the loose trousers to reveal a pair of taut buttocks and lean thighs. Quickly he slipped between the sheets, and soon the couple were embracing for the camera.

Transferring her gaze to the monitor, Lynne saw the actor caress the naked shoulders of his screen partner then cup her naked breast. She watched his fingers squeeze her large red nipple. The woman's face registered a quickening of desire, and Lynne found herself responding too. She was reminded of all the times she had gone to bed after an episode of *Night Owls* so turned on that she'd had to masturbate before she could sleep.

The kisses of the screen couple became more passionate and the quilt slipped down to reveal both torsos, Monica pressed hard against Hugo's hairy chest. Lynne, acutely aware of the tingling between her thighs, felt horribly voyeuristic but when she looked round everyone else seemed perfectly at ease. She supposed they must be used to it. After all, *Night Owls* was the raunchiest soap ever shown on British television.

The love scene stopped abruptly as the action was

cut, and then the pair lay back against the pillows, snuggling up to each other with supposedly post-coital affection. Lynne scanned the rugged features of the star and still couldn't quite believe that she would be dining with him that evening. Blake Harrison was forty-two (she'd looked that up in the TV yearbook) and a bit of a roughneck, but with irresistible charm, especially when he grinned. He was doing that now, as he looked down at his co-star and uttered the abominable cliché, 'Monica, darling, where have you been all my life?'

Once the take was over Lynne heard Blake exclaim, his words picked up by a nearby boom mike, 'Who the hell do they get to write these scripts – Barbara bloody Cartland?'

The floor manager called, 'That's a wrap, studio! Thanks very much everybody,' and Kate took Lynne's arm. 'We go to hospitality now, so you can meet His Majesty.'

'Fine. But I wouldn't mind going to the Ladies first.'

Lynne was relieved to have a few minutes alone. There had been people buzzing round her ever since two o'clock. Besides, she needed a chance to calm down after that torrid love scene. She could feel how wet she was between her legs and went into a cubicle to wipe away some of the excess. Lynne stared at her face in the cloakroom mirror and took some deep breaths. She was just about getting used to her new appearance.

She was changing inside, too. With a shock Lynne realised she was feeling sexy again. Nick's infidelity had depressed her libido for months, but now she was on a real high. Beneath the tight embrace of the revealing dress her breasts were swelling with arousal, hard nipples straining against the lacy cups, the silky French knickers mercifully cool against her skin. Lynne sighed, wondering what Nick would think of her now. Would he find her desirable, as he had in the beginning?

Debbi was in the hospitality suite with Don Chisholm, the director of *Night Owls*. 'So this is the lucky lady!' he grinned, holding out his big hand. 'Don't let Blake take you for a ride, will you? He's just like Hugo Townsend off the set. Type-casting!'

'Don't listen to him, Lynne,' Debbi smiled. 'He's been paying too much attention to the tabloids! Don, where are your manners? Aren't you going to offer our guest a drink?'

While Don was presiding at the drinks trolley Blake Harrison made his entrance, pausing to let everyone notice him. He wore a dark grey suit with a striped shirt and tasteful tie, and his dark, silver-streaked hair rose from his broad forehead in a sweeping style that brushed his shoulders. Now that he was without make-up, Lynne could see that his rather craggy face was lightly tanned.

His gaze homed in on her, the brown eyes widening briefly then narrowing again into their habitual half-closed position. Lynne knew he was examining every inch of her, and she could tell he liked what he saw. His wide mouth was set in the familiar down-turned smile that had given his character, Hugo, a reputation for cynicism, and a devil-may-care attitude towards women. Perhaps not even Blake himself could make the distinction any longer between his on-screen persona and his real self.

Don came out from behind the trolley. 'Blake, let me introduce you to Lynne Sanders.'

'Ah, Lynne! Congratulations on winning such a splendid prize!'

Blake's tone was self-mocking, and the rest of them laughed dutifully, as if they'd expected a joke. At his approach, Lynne could smell the musky spice aroma of Chanel's Antaeus cologne. His handshake lingered a few seconds longer than she expected. Their eyes met in a friendly smile, but she was aware that he was sizing her up. Was he wondering if she'd prove a boring dinner-companion? Or whether she'd be easy to talk into bed? Lynne felt a brief fluttering in the pit of her stomach at the realisation that soon she would be completely alone with him, for the rest of the evening.

Lynne relaxed once they were seated and the conversation was flowing easily between the actors. She found it fascinating just to eavesdrop on their post mortem of the day's work. Then the talk turned to discussion of the love-lives of various actors from another soap, produced in the same studio.

Engrossed in the gossip, Lynne was startled when Blake tapped her on the shoulder. 'Fascinating, isn't it, all this showbiz scandal?' he drawled. 'Unless you've heard it a million times before, of course. Would you object to us leaving now, Lynne? Table's booked for eight, but we could have a drink somewhere first. It's been a long, hard day and I've no great desire to remain on the premises any longer than I have to.'

'Of course!' Lynne got to her feet. 'I'll just say goodbye to Debbi and Kate.'

Debbi hugged her warmly. 'Have a wonderful evening, Lynne. You deserve it. And I'll be in touch about the photos soon.'

When Lynne was finally shepherded through the

swing doors and out into the cool evening air, she was gripped by panic. All her previous self-confidence seemed to drain away as she realised who she was with. What would people think when they saw them together? Suppose she ended up in the papers, labelled as Blake's latest conquest? What on earth would Nick think? Her husband knew nothing about the competition.

Then she realised, with a surge of defiance tinged with sadness, that it didn't matter what he thought. Their marriage was over. She could do anything she wanted now.

In the car park outside the studios was a beautiful silver Rolls. It was theirs for the evening, complete with chauffeur. Lynne sank back into the luxurious black leather upholstery with a small squeal of delight.

'San Marco's,' Blake told the driver. Smooth as a dream and quiet as a whisper, the limo whisked them out into the stream of traffic, which instantly gave way for them.

'I suppose this is what it's like to be rich and famous!' Lynne sighed.

'Don't ask me,' Blake grimaced. 'Famous I'll just about admit to, but "rich"? No way! I spent too long as a resting actor, working in burger joints, to qualify in that department.'

'So *Night Owls* gave you your big break then, did it?'

Blake shrugged. 'It's a living – of sorts. But don't let me spend all evening talking about myself, for heaven's sake. I'm far too big-headed as it is. I want to hear all about you, Lynne.'

He took her hand and squeezed it briefly. The back seat of the Rolls was wide and deep, allowing ample room for them both, but she was full of tremulous sexual excitement at being so near to such a charismatic and powerfully masculine figure. He was, quite unintentionally, making her feel like a gauche teenager again.

'Well, Lynne?' he prompted. 'First off, are you married?'

'Not really. Well, technically, yes, but we're in the process of splitting up.'

'Ah!' Blake sounded as if it was what he'd expected. His leonine head, with its long mane of silver hair, tipped back and he looked at her sideways. 'Any kids?'

'No, thank goodness. I suppose I never felt sure enough that it would last between me and Nick. Anyway, that's how I see it now.'

'How about work?'

'I'm between jobs right now. I was made redundant when the building society I worked for merged with a bank. I do some bar work, four nights a week. It pays the mortgage, but that's all.'

'Bar work, really? That's very interesting.'

Lynne couldn't imagine why, but there was no time to enquire as the car was coming to a smooth halt outside San Marco's restaurant in the King's Road.

Inside, Tim the barman welcomed Blake like an old friend. While he mixed Lynne a 'Manhattan Sunset' she glanced around. Everyone looked very smart and self-assured and some of the faces looked familiar, although she couldn't put a name to them. Her confidence began to wane.

'Come on, let's find a quiet corner,' Blake said, much to her relief.

Lynne was halfway through her second cocktail

and feeling decidedly woozy when Blake suddenly leaned forward, looked her closely in the eyes and said, 'Ever thought of getting into acting yourself?'

'No!' She was startled by the idea.

'Don't sound so horrified. It can be great fun, you know. I may have been slagging off a few people but overall the cast are great, I love 'em. And the production team. Anyway, what I'm leading up to is this. You remember Hazel? Sorry, you'll know her as June, the girl who works behind the bar in Hugo's club.'

'Oh yes. Short blonde hair, rather pretty.'

'That's her. Well, I'm sorry to say Hazel's a bit too fond of the old . . .' He lifted his elbow with a wink. 'Anyway, she's had her three warnings and I'm afraid she's for the chop. They're auditioning for a replacement, so why don't you try?'

'Me!'

'Yes, you!'

'But I told you, I've never done any acting before.'

'Neither had half the cast, I can assure you. As long as you can learn lines and you look the part, frankly that's all they require. Just a pretty face. You'd be spending the whole time behind the bar, so it wouldn't even matter if you had legs like tree-trunks.' He glanced down at her crossed thighs and Lynne clasped her hands over them nervously. 'Not that you have, of course. In fact you have extremely nice legs, and that dress shows them off beautifully. Now what was I saying, before I was so delightfully distracted? Oh yes, auditions. Why not give it a go? I'd put in a good word for you with Don. He likes you already, I can tell. You're halfway there.'

Lynne was finding it hard to take in. Mixing with

television people for a few hours was one thing, but she'd never dreamed of doing it for a living. Yet would Blake have mentioned it if he didn't think she could do it?

'Well, you don't have to decide now,' Blake smiled, taking her hand and pulling her to her feet. 'I think our table's ready.'

The San Marco restaurant had an ambience of quiet elegance and the low lighting and positioning of the tables in alcoves behind banks of plants ensured privacy. Lynne couldn't help wondering how many discreet liaisons had been carried on there by all kinds of celebrities – perhaps even Royalty!

'This is the place where rich men bring their mistresses, never their wives,' Blake commented, echoing her thoughts. Lynne found herself blushing and lowered her eyes to the menu. She felt out of her depth and was grateful for the exotic plants that hid her from general view. At least people wouldn't spot her there with Blake and wonder who she was.

Even so, when she glanced down at her pink dress, and remembered her new make-up and hairstyle, Lynne realised that she didn't look at all out of place as Blake's dinner companion. In fact, they probably looked rather good together. Once she had become used to the idea she felt a surge of self-confidence.

'Champagne, madam?'

Lynne nodded as the waiter filled her glass with sizzling bubbles. She was already feeling the effects of the two cocktails. But what the hell? Tonight was special, and she was determined to make the most of it.

The meal was perfectly cooked and beautifully

presented, but Lynne hardly tasted the food as they went through four courses. She was experiencing it all through a glorious haze, listening to Blake telling her about his travels in the West Indies and South America, grateful that she wasn't expected to do any more than nod and smile. By the end of the evening she felt as if she were in some wonderful paradise of the senses, far removed from anything as petty and annoying as redundancy or divorce. She didn't even have to worry about getting home, because the Rolls was still parked outside the restaurant.

'Since this wonderful vehicle is all ours for the evening, why don't we go on a little jaunt?' Blake suggested, as they settled into the back seat again. 'Take us on a tour of Mayfair!' he called.

Driving through the most glamorous areas of London, streets full of light and optimism, Lynne felt on top of the world. Blake had his arm along the seat behind her now, and she leant back against it, cautiously. He was very comfortable to be with, she decided, easy to talk to. Yet she was well aware of the undercurrent of animal energy beneath his laid-back exterior. She was being drawn to him physically, her body already in a state of semi-arousal, her mind too dazzled by the amazing events of the day to put up much resistance to the overwhelming effect his nearness was having on her senses.

'Well, have you enjoyed your day?' she heard him ask in a low voice very near her ear.

She could feel his warm breath on her cheeks as she answered, 'Oh yes, it's been wonderful! Absolutely wonderful!'

'Good. So how would you like to round it off then, Lynne?'

Was she imagining it? No, his lips really were touching the sensitive lobe of her ear, sending waves of excitement careering through her veins. She froze, answering in a whisper, 'I suppose I'd better be getting home.'

'And where might "home" be?'

Lynne told him the name of her road in Ealing and he relayed it to the driver. Lynne could feel Blake's hand on her shoulder, heavy and warm. He was right beside her now, his lean thigh pressing against hers, and the unmistakable heat of desire was kindling within her. The short skirt had ridden up, exposing far too much of her dark stocking top, and Blake's frequent downward glances told her that he found the sight alluring.

Suddenly he murmured, 'Ever made love in a Rolls Royce before, Lynne?'

The driver's face in the mirror was expressionless. With her heart thumping out a warning Lynne began to protest, 'I've never even . . .' but Blake's arms were encircling her and his mouth closed in, meeting hers with persuasive force. For a moment Lynne wondered whether she should kick him in the shins, but she had no desire to behave so churlishly. Blake's lips were softening against hers and she savoured their moist fullness, telling herself that this was Blake Harrison, *the* Blake Harrison, and he really was kissing her. Not as 'Hugo' but as himself, and for real. It still seemed incredible.

His mouth moved away, but only so that he could murmur, 'Lynne, this has been the nicest evening I've had for ages. You're the sexiest woman I've met in a long time.'

Blake resumed their kiss with renewed passion, and the effect was even more intoxicating than that of champagne. His tongue was probing eagerly, meeting hers halfway, and with his free hand he was stroking her smooth, Lycra-clad thigh. Reaching the top of her stockings he let just one finger stray beneath and wormed his way down against her bare skin. Lynne shuddered voluptuously at the contact, and felt herself moistening in the hidden place, just inches from his hand, where her desire was keenest.

Their tongues were entwined sensually now, and as the kiss deepened Lynne felt her inhibitions melt away in the glorious warmth that was spreading to all corners of her body. She could feel the yearning thrust of her breasts and the insistent throbbing between her thighs that made her want more, yet more, of this delicious stimulation. Blake managed to unclip her suspender, rolling down her stocking so that all of one thigh was exposed. Then he made tantalising strokes up and down the sensitive inner flesh, stopping short of her silk knickers, making her groan with urgent longing.

His mouth left hers and began to trace a path down her neck while one hand opened her jacket, exposing her bosom. At once his lips went to the divide between her breasts and he probed between them with his tongue, sending new erotic signals through her overloaded system. With a faint cry, Lynne sank back in utter abandon until her head was resting on the seat. Dimly aware that Blake had come to kneel on the floor beside her, she pulled her rucked skirt up around her waist to allow him easier access. While he continued his licking of her cleavage one hand was unclipping the other suspender, tickling the skin of her inner thighs as he did so. He found the button that secured her knickers and soon the garment was sliding down her hips, revealing her downy mons beneath the frilly garter belt, sliding down over her knees to end up round her ankles.

Arching her body, Lynne felt behind her back for her zipper and inched it down until she could slip the top of the dress over her shoulders. She no longer cared what the chauffeur could see in his mirror. Blake helped her, giving a low moan as her bra became visible, filled to overflowing with her ripe flesh. Greedily he pushed down one of the lacy cups and took her aching nipple in his mouth, rolling it around with his tongue until she squirmed with delight, feeling the powerful currents of sensation join up with those already flowing from below.

She could feel his fingers brushing her pubic hair and, sighing, kicked the silky panties off her feet then let her thighs fall loosely apart. His hand reached her moistening sex, finding the source of her greatest pleasure and stroking delicately with his fingertip. His ministrations made her juices flow copiously, and she heard him give another moan and release her swollen nipple from his mouth. Slowly he traversed her body, first kissing the taut underside of her breast, then mouthing his way down the plane of her stomach as far as her navel. After a while he dived beneath the bunched material at her hips so that he could nuzzle softly in her warm fuzz.

Lynne, knowing exactly where his lips were heading, felt a keen thrill of anticipation. His finger had moved to her labia now and was probing gently. She tightened her vulva over it, striving to wring as much pleasure as she could from the tentative contact. She needed him to be firmer with her now, rougher even.

Then, to her extreme satisfaction, his mouth moved down the last few inches to fasten on her jutting clitoris. He began to lick it rapidly, and the resulting reverberations notched up her arousal by several degrees. Looking down at the familiar head of Hugo, the randy nightclub owner, Lynne felt as if she were starring in an episode of the soap. She began to fantasise about performing in front of the camera, had lustful thoughts of him screwing her while millions watched, making her sex convulse with acute desire.

Soon Blake was giving her streaming pussy his full attention and Lynne was loving every second. It was so long since she'd felt this turned on. She'd almost forgotten how it felt to be giving herself up to pleasure, revelling in the powerful feelings that were sweeping her towards ultimate satisfaction. His fingers were right inside her now, filling her up entirely, while his mouth continued to work at her engorged clitoris, sending increasing thrills all over the surface of her body and reverberations deep within, bringing her towards the first climax she'd had in months that was not self-induced.

The exquisite rippling waves were making her moan as Blake kissed her upturned nipple, increasing her rapture. Lynne was caught in a timeless web of ecstasy, her whole body vibrating on a new and wonderful wavelength, helping her to feel whole and empowered once again. At last she felt the intensity fading, drawing her back down towards a state of dreamy exhaustion and complete satiation.

Dimly she was aware of Blake pulling her

knickers back on, fastening her suspenders, zipping up her dress. Lynne submitted with child-like passivity, but the void left by her spent passion was filled with growing unease. Now the heat of the moment was over, she was afraid to face the reality she dreaded: the fact that Blake Harrison, a soap star with a reputation for womanising, had just gone down on her in the back of a Rolls.

It occurred to her that women had made the front page of the tabloids for being caught in similar situations. All the bliss abruptly evaporated and she was left with a feeling of shame. She'd let it all go to her head – the sudden transformation of her appearance, being treated like a celebrity, riding in a Rolls – but the end result had been an undignified backseat petting session, made even more distasteful by its predictability.

'This is your road, Lynne,' she heard Blake say in a matter-of-fact tone. 'What number shall I tell the chauffeur?'

'Thirty-seven,' Lynne mumbled. As the car slowed, she looked at Blake. He was sitting there faintly smiling, not a hair out of place. Lynne badly wanted to believe that their encounter had meant something to him, but her heart told her otherwise. She saw him reach into his inside pocket and draw out a card. He scrawled something on the back and handed it to her. 'There you are. Next Tuesday, ten a.m. Don't forget now, will you?'

She stared at him, still in a daze. He leaned over and gave her a lingering kiss on the mouth that, despite herself, revived earlier feelings until the car finally slowed to a halt. As he drew back he smiled rather fondly, making her feel a bit better.

'Thanks for a lovely evening,' she said, her words

sounding hollow to her ears.

'No, thank *you*, Lynne,' Blake insisted. His words sounded sincere until she remembered that he was, after all, an actor.

Chapter Two

NEXT DAY, WHEN Lynne reflected on what had occurred in the back of the Rolls, she decided she had over-reacted. Her jaded mood after the event had probably resulted from coming down after all that champagne. She couldn't deny she'd enjoyed the experience immensely while it was happening. Furthermore, it had reminded her of what sex could be like. The last few years with Nick had steadily eroded her libido until she'd just lost the urge. Well, at least she now knew that she could enjoy making love again.

Not that she'd exactly 'made love' with Blake. Although I wouldn't mind, Lynne told herself dreamily, as she gazed into the bathroom mirror. Devoid of make-up she had the same features as before, but the new hairstyle was still there and she decided she was going to keep it. She liked the way it made her look: younger than her twenty-five years, bright and slightly cheeky. Maybe she should grow a personality to match, have some fun for a change.

On Tuesday morning she entered the doors of

Sphere TV again, already feeling almost at home there despite her nervousness. What if she did join the cast of *Night Owls*, would she make a go of it? Blake had assured ther that little acting experience was necessary, but Lynne was doubtful. Still, if he had put in a good word for her maybe she was in with a chance.

She was directed to the hospitality room for coffee and given some lines to learn. There were eight other women waiting to audition for the part of the barmaid, and Lynne's confidence was sapped as she overheard them talking about their previous parts and other auditions. One by one they were called through a door at the far end and never seen again. Then, at long last, it was Lynne's turn.

Don recognised her at once and smiled a welcome. 'Hello again, Lynne. Did you enjoy your day with us?'

'Very much, thanks.'

'When Blake suggested we should audition you I agreed straight away. I'm not making any promises, mind.'

He pointed to a corner of the studio where the 'bar' was set up. Slowly they both walked over to it, and Lynne peered at the pumps, drip trays and optics. 'Looks pretty authentic to me,' she smiled.

'Yes, Blake said you'd worked in a pub. That should help you pitch it right with the manner, the actions and so on. What we'd like to do, Lynne, is run through a short scene between you and Jonathan here, who plays Andrew Carr.'

The actor stepped forward and Lynne recognised his mop of fair hair and rather boyish features at once, although he looked thinner than on the screen. She tentatively held out her hand and he shook it firmly, his blue eyes glinting warmly. Lynne was hoping she wouldn't forget her lines, but there was nothing much to it: 'Andrew' ordered a pint, she poured it and took his money, then they had a bit of a chat about the weather. But, after that, Don wanted them to improvise for a while, just to see if Lynne could get the feel of the part. That was the bit that terrified her.

Once Jonathan began, however, Lynne relaxed into it. She was familiar enough with the soap to know both his character and that of the barmaid, while the actions of pulling the pint and giving change were second nature to her. She managed to speak her half dozen lines without fluffing any of them, and when it came to continuing their conversation Lynne found she could pretend she was serving behind the bar of the Red Lion. All the old clichés came tripping off her tongue. Once she got warmed up she could continue for hours, and it was only when Don shouted 'Cut!' that she realised where she was.

'Wow, I got really carried away there!' she confessed, blushing.

'No problem, that was great!' Don assured her. 'Look, would you mind waiting for me through that door over there? Just for a few minutes.'

As she walked away Jonathan touched her elbow and whispered, 'Well done!' It gave Lynne a boost, but she wasn't counting any chickens. Although she'd lost her nerves and ended up enjoying the audition it still didn't mean she was going to be right for the part. Someone else might have done better.

Lynne waited in the small ante-room with three actresses for what seemed like ages. Presumably they were all shortlisted. At last Don opened the door, followed by his assistant with the inevitable clipboard.

'Sorry to keep you, but we have come to a decision now,' Don began briskly. 'We've decided to give the part to Lynne Sanders.'

While she was being congratulated, and the other girls were being dismissed with thanks for coming and best wishes for the future, Lynne's mind was reeling incredulously. Behind her elation, however, was a nagging doubt. Would Blake have recommended her for the part if she hadn't let him have his way with her in the back of the Rolls?

'I'm sure you'll be ideal as June's replacement,' Don was saying.

They went down the corridor to an office where she was introduced to a woman called Maggie, who went through the terms of the contract. It was very exciting, but also bewildering, and by the time they'd finished with her Lynne just wanted to be alone. After leaving Sphere TV she went straight home. She had to read over her contract to make quite sure she knew its contents, sign it and post it back to Maggie before the job was really hers. Then she'd be sent her script and asked to attend a briefing meeting in a week's time. Hazel, the actress who played June, had been taken into a drying out clinic so they'd had to write her out of the soap in a hurry.

That evening, Blake phoned. 'Congratulations! I knew you were right for the part but Don was even more impressed than I'd expected. He said you were a natural. Anyway, how about coming to dinner with me tomorrow night, by way of celebration?'

'I'd love to!' Lynne declared. Even the sound of his voice affected her like champagne. When she found out that she was invited to his flat in Hampstead, however, her excitement took on a subtly different quality. Did he intend to carry on making love where they'd left off? It certainly looked like it. The thought sent a tingling warmth flowing through her veins.

After putting the phone down she danced round the room, full of euphoria. It was incredible; her life was getting more and more exciting. And right there in the heart of it all was gorgeous, irresistible Blake Harrison. Was she going to have a full-blown affair with him? The idea seemed less incredible every minute. He had taken her under his wing because he liked her, fancied her, and soon they'd be making love again. Her luck had certainly changed when she'd entered that competition.

Lynne reflected on how Nick might react to her latest success. For years her husband had held her back, persuaded her to take a job in a building society instead of returning to college. Well, now she was doing all right for herself and the future looked bright. Once their divorce was through she could really forget the past and start again.

On Wednesday night, Lynne spent some time wondering what to wear. In the bottom of her underwear drawer she found the sexy black lace bra she'd bought to try to spice up her love-life with Nick. She hadn't succeeded, but it wasn't for want of trying. Holding up the garment she remembered that it was little more than a sling support for her breasts which produced a good cleavage but left her nipples completely exposed. With a thrill of anticipation she shrugged off her bathrobe and tried the bra on. The blatant eroticism of her bared breasts and jutting nipples made her look like a stripper. Rummaging in her drawer again she found its companion: a minuscule scrap of lace that went round her hips and decorated her groin with a black frill but left her crotch completely open.

Feeling deliciously wicked, Lynne put on the crotchless panties and matching black suspender belt. She tried on her one black dress but then decided to wear a pale blue one with a low, round neck that revealed the outline of her nipples more clearly. There was no point in wearing such a bra otherwise. Aware that she had gone out of her way to appear seductive Lynne left the house in a mood of heady elation.

That same mood persuaded her to hang the expense and take a taxi all the way from Ealing to the Hampstead address Blake had given her. She suspected she'd have no desire to drive home after the night of unbridled passion she was anticipating. Besides, it made her feel special. Soon she would no longer be plain Lynne Sanders: she would also be Carol, the new barmaid, from *Night Owls*. The very idea of it still made her shiver with excitement.

Blake came to the door of his flat with a wooden spoon in his hand, much to Lynne's amusement. Savoury smells wafted from the kitchen, mixing with his cologne.

'I never thought of you as a chef!' she grinned as he kissed her cheek.

'Aha, hidden talents! I've rustled up something rather special for us this evening, just wait and see! But first, I'm going to make you one of my special champagne cocktails. It isn't every week I get such a charming new co-star as you!'

'Hardly a star!' Lynne protested modestly.

'Everyone in *Night Owls* is a star, as you'll soon find out. You'll be seeing yourself in "Soaplines" magazine before you know it.'

'Oh dear, I do hope not.'

'Why?' Blake stared at her for a few moments, his hooded grey eyes surveying her seriously. 'Don't you want to be famous?'

'I'm not sure I'm ready for it.'

'Then you'd better get used to the idea double quick. Or if you can't stand the heat, get out of the kitchen. Which reminds me, I must get back to mine. Put something melodious on the stereo – I'll be with you in a moment.'

Lynne found a Sinatra album and put that on, then settled back into the Victorian style deep-button sofa. The large living-room was furnished in traditional style, with a dining table set with candelabra and roses at one end. There was a vast Nicam TV set in a unit which also contained video and CD players, next to a large cocktail cabinet. Lynne had the impression that Blake entertained a lot. She began to fantasise about the people who had been in that room: most of the cast of *Night Owls*, presumably, and maybe other actors as well. It dawned on her that, through Blake, she might meet all kinds of famous people.

He returned with a smile, and proceeded to fix her the cocktail he'd promised. It tasted of brandy and orange juice, as well as champagne, and the first sip turned Lynne light-headed.

'Here's to your new career as an actress!' Blake smiled, raising his glass.

Lynne took another sip but then felt Blake's lips on hers, sensual, persuasive. Not that she needed much persuading. He stepped back from her with a wink and held up his outspread fingers. 'This is just an aperitif! Five minutes, then we can start the feast.'

His tone was full of innuendo, fuelling her hopes that they would end up in bed together before the evening was out. During the next five minutes Lynne felt her whole body tuning up for pleasure. She could smell the delicious aromas from the food and her mouth began to water. The relaxing, seductive music was putting her in a languorous mood, and she absently stroked the velvet cushion she was resting against. Memories of how she felt when Blake had caressed her and finally given her the satisfaction she craved were filling her head, making her breasts expand and evoking flutters of erotic awakening deep inside her. Restlessly she crossed her thighs and felt the tingling warmth in her crotch intensify.

By the time Blake entered with the first course, Lynne was on a sexual high. Perhaps suspecting as much he drew her into his arms before they began the meal and gave her a luscious kiss on the mouth, sending powerful currents of arousal swirling through her. When he withdrew she felt dizzy, holding on to the back of a chair for support.

'You look wonderful, Lynne,' Blake smiled as they took their places. 'Something tells me you're going to become a great favourite with the viewers – and probably with the cast, too.'

'I do hope so, but I'm very nervous,' she admitted. 'I've been thinking, is Carol likely to get any love scenes? I mean ordinary acting is difficult enough, but if I had to take my clothes off in front of a million viewers I'd be so embarrassed. Frankly, Blake, I don't think I could do it.'

He laughed. 'Nonsense! There's nothing to it

really, once you've done it a couple of times. Just remember it's all an illusion. You saw how we did it the other day, didn't you? A few gropes in the buff then they cut the scene and next thing it's supposed to be all over. We're not making porno movies, you know.'

Lynne blushed. 'Yes, but it's easy for you to talk.'

They began to eat the Japanese-style avocado salad, which Lynne pronounced delicious. Blake said, 'Look, if you want to rehearse love scenes I'm happy to oblige. I can show you a few hints and tips, make you feel more confident. Would that help?'

Lynne reacted with a jolt in the pit of her stomach. It might help my acting career, Lynne thought as she nodded her assent, but it's not helping my digestion! The idea of making love with Blake Harrison, whether for 'practice' or for real, was setting disturbing currents in motion throughout her body.

Blake began telling her how his career as a TV chef was cut short when the company was taken over by Sphere. He was offered a part in *Night Owls* as compensation.

'Not that I mind,' he grinned. 'The way I look at it, there's dozens of other chefs on television but only one Hugo Townsend. I always wanted an acting career, and the cookery only came about because I was running my own restaurant and media types used to eat there.'

The more he talked about himself, the more Lynne realised what a fascinating man he was. He'd learnt to cook on a cruise liner, and had even catered for Hollywood stars. But, as he freely admitted, he'd spent all his money on high living and returned to England penniless, having to work in restaurant kitchens to survive.

'Well, I've certainly profited from your experience tonight,' Lynne smiled, after lingering over the last mouthful of chestnut soufflé. 'That was the most delicious meal I've ever had.'

'Good. Shall we take our coffee sitting on the sofa?'

Once they were seated near each other Lynne felt a reckless wave of desire come over her. She longed to throw herself into his brawny arms, to abandon herself to those sensitive fingers and searching lips, to let him fulfil the promise of their previous encounter.

'Brandy?' he offered.

'No, thank you, Blake. I think I've had enough alcohol.'

She watched him pour himself a generous measure, feeling delightfully mellow. The strong male scent of him was almost overwhelming her, but she didn't know how much was artificial and how much was natural. If there were such things as pheromones, she reflected, they must each be sending them out in droves right now!

Casually Blake put his arm around her as he settled back in the sofa, increasing her longing for more intimate contact. She kicked off her shoes, put her feet up on the seat beside her and snuggled close to him. He planted a kiss on her forehead, then drained his glass. Soon he was kissing her in earnest, his tongue penetrating into her willing mouth, filling it with the fruity aftertaste of his drink. Their kiss became deeper, more passionate. But, just as she was feeling totally abandoned, he drew back from her.

'Tell you what, let's pretend this is a scene from the soap. Here we are in Hugo's flat, and you've already had far too much to drink. But you still feel that perhaps you shouldn't give in to this Don Juan everyone's warned you about. So what do you do?'

Lynne felt confused. The scenario sounded altogether too realistic. 'I . . . I don't know.'

'Let's consider your options. You can either slap his face and leave. Or, you might tell him you've already got a boyfriend. Try to put a stop to his advances without hurting his feelings. I would guess that's what Carol would do, because she'd want to keep her job behind the bar.'

'And what if she decided to go along with it?'

'Aha!' Blake's grey eyes brightened. 'In that case, we go into the big love scene. Another few seconds on the sofa, then I whisper in your ear and we go off, hand in hand, into the bedroom. Usually they would cut the action there, ready to pick it up again later. Maybe not until the next episode.'

Lynne nodded, unsure what to do about her mounting frustration. Were they going to end up in bed, or weren't they? Then she realised that was exactly what the director would want the viewers to feel. She gave a wry smile. 'Okay. Let's go for the love scene, then.'

Blake gave the slow, insinuating smile that was already capable of driving her to distraction. He kissed her again, this time with infinite tenderness. 'Oh, Carol!' he murmured. 'The moment I set eyes on you I started longing for this moment.'

'Me too,' Lynne giggled.

Blake gave her a stern look. 'But are you sure, quite sure, that this is what you want?'

'Oh, yes!'

'Cut!' He took her hand and pulled her towards the door. 'Next scene, in bed together.'

'Really? That soon?'

'Of course. Remember, a week could have passed in real time since that last take. Meanwhile the viewer is left in suspense, wondering just how much of the action they're going to show this time. Will it be as good as that scene between Andrew and Penny, where he stripped the clothes off her one by one? Or will it be a bit of a teaser like the one with Sam and Laura where, just as it got interesting, Laura's husband burst in and spoilt the fun? See what I mean?'

Lynne certainly did. She had been there herself, as a regular viewer, kept on the edge of her seat by such questions as those. And, as Blake led her through into his bedroom, she was wondering right now just how far their 'scene' would go.

First he laid her gently down on the king-size bed, with its peach satin sheets, and began kissing her with renewed passion. His fingers found her nipples, roused and prominent beneath the silky cloth, and she was gratified to see his eyebrows raised.

'Rule number one: don't conceal the interesting bits from the camera,' he murmured, stroking her uplifted breast. Lynne sighed, thrusting her chest high and wiggling her hips in voluptuous arousal. His hand moved to the smoothness of her skirt and he proceeded to stroke her mons through the tight-fitting material.

'Rule two, don't leave too long a gap in the dialogue or the viewers will think there's something wrong with their TV set!' He continued in his 'smoothie' voice, 'Carol, darling, if I told you that you have the most exquisite body, would you hold it against me?'

Lynne giggled despite herself, then groaned. 'This isn't exactly turning me on you know, Blake. In fact, I'd say quite the opposite.'

'Precisely.' He began to pull down the zipper of her dress. 'I'm giving you a taste of the real thing. This is how we carry on in the studio, much of the time. I mean, can you imagine what would happen if we took the sex scenes seriously?'

Lynne saw his point, but she couldn't help feeling let down. Was this to be just a demonstration of acting techniques, after all?

Blake was pulling down her dress, exposing the pale mounds of her breasts, his eyes widening as he realised what kind of bra she was wearing. He continued easing it over her hips and down her thighs. She helped to free herself until she lay almost completely nude, wearing only the slinky black triangle that covered her pubis. Blake sat back on his haunches and surveyed her from head to foot.

'Gorgeous!' he declared, his normally hooded eyes opening wide and bright. His head ducked to her thigh, where he kissed her several times, brushing his lips tentatively over the sensitive skin and reviving Lynne's waning desire. She felt him traverse the sliver of satin below her hip and kiss his way along her left side, ending at the lower slope of her breast. At the same time his right hand was caressing her other thigh, sweeping up until his palm brushed the lacy frill that barely covered her labia, then returning to her knee again.

'Well, I think this is about as far as the censor would let us go,' Blake announced, after his tongue had flitted several times across the ripe cone of her nipple. 'Usually the director would leave the rest to the viewer's imagination.'

Lynne stared into his impassive face and wondered what to make of him. Was this just some cruel cat-and-mouse game he was playing?

Then his cheeks creased into a smile and he gave her nipple a playful nip with the edge of his teeth. 'But we don't have to stop there, do we? We can go on being naughty people doing dirty things. It looks like you're dressed for the part!'

'Mm! What you were doing just then was very nice indeed,' Lynne told him, relieved that the play-acting seemed to be over. Maybe now she would get some real satisfaction.

Lynne could feel his chest pressed against her side, hard and uncompromising. The desire was growing in her to become better acquainted with his body, to know just what he was like under his clothes, and she began to undo the buttons of his shirt. Her flat palms found their way in, feeling the solid, moulded flesh with its sprinkling of hairs, but the shirt remained on his back. She kissed both of the tiny, rigid nipples in turn.

Blake dodged away from her and slid down her body again. He began to mouth her pussy through the thin stuff of her panties, making her squirm with sudden hunger. Soon, though, his lips returned to her breast and his finger crept down beneath her waistband to insinuate itself into the darkness of her sex. Lynne parted her legs wide, allowing him to plunge right into her and feel the pulsating depths of her vagina through her wicked panties. She squeezed down on him hard, loving the sudden fierce contact between his wrist and the throbbing centre of her sexuality.

He came out of her and she realised how very wet she was. The place between her thighs was all liquid now, flooded with her passion, and he began to stroke her deliciously from one end to the other, pressing on her clitoris when he reached the top and then, at the other end, just teasing the puckered mouth of her anus with the tip of his finger. The area around her sex was highly aroused and Lynne kept wiggling her hips, hoping to trap his finger inside her as he slid past on his slippery path. When she succeeded she sighed with contentment. But then he would sneak out again and her longing would redouble, so that she became increasingly desperate for the penetration she craved.

Lynne reached out and found the zipper of Blake's fly. Hoping he would take the hint she began to slide it down, but he removed her hand and wriggled out of her reach. Once his fingers were inside her again she forgot all about trying to seduce him in the sweet delirium of having her own needs served.

Blake began licking her swollen nub while he fingered her sex, taking her with expert precision towards a climax that she knew would surpass even the one she had experienced in the Rolls. She could feel it gathering momentum, propelling her towards the final surge of wild pleasure from which there would be no turning back. Losing all inhibition she worked her hips frantically to get the satisfaction she needed, urging his tongue to work her more strongly, sighing with relief when he took her cue and thrust into her with his bunched fingers, giving her the deeper penetration she hungered for. Avidly her vagina strove to extract every bit of keen sensation through its squeezing walls.

When her orgasm finally arrived it took her by surprise with its sheer power. Time and again she felt herself clench Blake's delving fingers as the ripples surged through her with a seismic force, sending hot reverberations through her body. The moments were tense and tightly focused, reaching an almost unbearable acuteness before they began to diminish, leaving her drained and numb.

'Oh God!' she breathed, falling back into the downy nest of the duvet. 'That was amazing!'

He kissed her on the forehead, then rose and left the room. Too exhausted to raise her head she lay with eyes closed, her body in a state of total relaxation, until she fell asleep.

Lynne was roused by Blake's voice and his touch upon her shoulder. 'Come on, Lynne, wakey, wakey!' Drowsily she opened her eyes and stared up at him. 'I brought you a drink of fizzy water. After all that alcohol you'll need it. Come on, sweetheart, sit up and take a sip. You'll feel better soon.'

Bleary-eyed she took some of the chilled, sparkling water. It seemed to work instantly, making her feel more alert. Blake's face came into focus, his grey eyes surveying her thoughtfully, his wide mouth in a half-smile. Then he spoke to her in a slow, deliberate tone.

'Look, Lynne, it's almost one a.m. and I've phoned for a taxi to take you home. I have to get up at five to be at the studio by six, so I must snatch a few hours' sleep and if you stayed I don't believe I'd get any! I hope you don't mind.'

'No,' she mumbled hazily. 'That's okay.'

'Maybe you should give your face a splash. Bathroom's through there.'

While she was in there Lynne heard the doorbell and knew the taxi had arrived. She was still half asleep and faintly bewildered, but she scrambled into her clothes nevertheless and in a few minutes was ready to go. Blake gave her a hug and kissed her tenderly on the lips.

'Thanks for a lovely evening,' she burbled.

'My pleasure. See you at the studio, if not before. Bye now, Lynne. Safe journey home.'

She fell asleep in the taxi and had to be revived by the driver, but once she was home it was a relief to finally slip into her own bed. Sleep did not come straight away, however. Her sleep pattern had been thoroughly disrupted and she lay awake for some time.

Lynne couldn't get Blake out of her mind. Twice now he had made one-sided love to her without even taking off his clothes. Didn't he want some of the action for himself? Maybe he was being a gentleman, she told herself, not wanting to push himself on her too soon. It was a nice thought, but somehow it didn't ring true. Maybe there was a more sinister explanation, like he had Aids or something. Lynne shuddered: she did hope not. Already she could feel herself growing fond of him. Well, time would tell if their relationship was going to develop physically, or in any other way. One thing was sure: her life would be transformed from now on. Sighing with pleasure at the thought of all the excitement that lay ahead, Lynne turned into her favourite position for sleep.

Chapter Three

'OKAY, IT'S A wrap everyone! Thanks, studio.'

Lynne had never heard such welcome words in her life. It was the end of her first day on *Night Owls* and the strain had begun to tell. Although she only had three lines to deliver, she'd frozen completely on one of the takes and they'd had to shoot it all again.

But now it was over and the roof hadn't fallen in; neither had she been sacked. In fact, Don made a point of congratulating her as the actors filed off the set. 'Well, you've survived!' he grinned. 'Lynne, you did really well. I knew you wouldn't let me down.'

'It's kind of you to say so.'

Don gave her a serious look for a moment. 'Lynne, just remember this: I don't do "kind". I'm not into bolstering egos. Just you make sure you're as good next time, okay?'

When she got to the bar, Blake was deep in conversation with someone else and Lynne found herself talking to Jonathan instead. 'How do you feel?' he asked her. 'Relieved?'

'I should say so! Honestly, I've never been so

scared in my life. Then, when my mind went blank in the middle of that scene, I wanted to die.'

'It's happened to all of us, at least once,' he assured her. 'The important thing is not to dwell on it. I'm sure you'll be fine, Lynne, once you get used to the routine.'

'When will the scene we did today be shown, do you know?'

'Friday week. That's if we're not re-scheduled for a football match. It has been known!'

Lynne didn't linger in the bar. She felt utterly drained and wanted to get home as soon as possible so she could go through her lines then have an early night.

Next morning Lynne expected to see Blake again, but he wasn't needed that day. Somehow she felt extra nervous not having him around. His friendly face had seen her through the trials of the first day, but now she would have to manage alone.

Not quite alone, however. Jonathan was in the same scene, and gave her as much of his support as he could. Their characters had a conversation at the bar, and it was quite a flirty one, even though 'Andrew' already had a long-term girlfriend called Penny. Sandra Woods, who played Penny, had to appear halfway through the scene.

'Lynne, do you think you could unbutton that blouse a bit more?' the director suggested after the first run-through. 'I want you to look more seductive at the point where Penny walks in. Lean over the bar, show a bit more cleavage. That's better!'

It was the first time Lynne had been called on to act sexily, and she was very self-conscious. But she knew she had to do it in order to make the rest of the scene seem credible.

'Don't worry,' Jonathan said as she tentatively undid another button. 'I've seen it all before!'

Lynne giggled, feeling easier, then pushed her breasts together as she rested her arms on the bar. Even so, it made her feel strange to behave so blatantly. She'd never have done so in real life but that, she reminded herself, was just what acting was all about. Maybe I'll end up being a real actress after all, she thought wryly, as they prepared to go through it once more.

'When Hugo told me he'd hired a smashing new barmaid, I thought he meant you kept breaking glasses,' Jonathan grinned, acting as Andrew, his eyes fastened on her cleavage. Lynne groaned. Then he stared straight into her eyes, and she felt her pulse quicken for real. 'But I think you're more likely to break hearts, Carol,' he continued, slurring his words. He was supposed to have drunk six pints. 'Are you a heart-breaker, my lovely? Or are you a ball-breaker? 'Cause if you are . . .'

'So *there* you are, Andrew! Surprise, surprise!'

As the jealous girlfriend appeared, Lynne turned her back on the couple and went to serve another customer. She was supposed to overhear them arguing over her while maintaining her cool. It wasn't easy, but when the scene was over Jonathan congratulated her.

'I think you'll be pleased when you see yourself on TV,' he smiled.

It was an experience that Lynne was both looking forward to and dreading.

She had no more to do for a week, and to be suddenly plunged into idleness after all that frantic activity was a bit of a let-down. It was also strange that she'd heard nothing from Blake. Lynne had been expecting at least a phone call, but when she finally gained the courage to ring him all she got was his answerphone. Had he decided to drop her, now she was in the programme? Maybe he'd lost interest in her, but he might at least have rung to see how she'd got on. Still, she wasn't in love with him. The sex had been very nice, and had reawakened some dormant urges, but she wasn't going to lose any sleep over him.

The days began to drag, and evenings even more so. Lynne had given up her bar job because she couldn't guarantee to be there on the same nights each week. After a day in the studio there was no way she could spend the evening working. But she'd told Jackie, the landlady, that she would still be available on a casual basis. So when she had a call asking her to help out in the Red Lion on Thursday, for a stag night, Lynne was glad of the diversion.

'How's it going?' Jackie asked as soon as Lynne arrived.

Lynne grimaced. 'It's harder than real bar work, I can tell you!'

'When are we going to see you on the box then?'

'Tomorrow night. To be honest, I'm dreading it. I've not even told my Mum yet, let alone my ex. I suppose they're bound to find out sooner or later.'

'Better tell them sooner, love, before you're splashed all over the front of "Soaplines".'

The bar began to fill with boisterous young men out on a spree. Lynne was used to it, but when a strippergram girl arrived the atmosphere became so riotous that she grew nervous. There were only three of them behind the bar that night, and Jackie was already half drunk as usual, but fortunately the two barmen were dependable types.

The men in the stag party were clapping and stamping as the pretty blonde girl began taking off her clothes. She was making a play for the groom, a stupid-looking bloke called Gerry, and he was drooling over her. His mates were egging him on and the situation was getting heavy. Although the girl continued to smile and gyrate in her bra and pants, there was a scared look in her eyes.

'Jackie, it's getting out of hand,' Lynne warned, but the landlady ignored her.

Suddenly Gerry and his mates pushed the girl on to a table. She screamed, but the barmen were so busy serving they didn't notice. From where she was standing, Lynne could see quite clearly that two of the men were pulling down the girl's pants while Gerry unzipped himself. She rushed out from behind the bar, calling to the others as she did so, 'Jim! Bob! Come and help this poor girl, for God's sake. She doesn't deserve this!'

The men at the table turned towards her, leering and jeering. Then came the landlady's unmistakable voice. 'Hey, lads, guess who this is? She's a celebrity! Out of that soap *Night Birds*. Would you believe, she plays a barmaid! She's only slumming it in here tonight. Tomorrow she'll be on the telly!'

Although Jackie's words had the desired effect in diverting the men's attention, Lynne was horrified. She saw the stripper take her chance and roll off the table, scrambling away and out of the door, but now she had to face the mob herself. Aware that her heart was thudding painfully, she tried her best to stay calm.

'Is that true?' gawped Gerry, bleary-eyed.

Lynne tried not to sound too scared, aiming for a nonchalant tone. 'It's only a small part. Just a barmaid, like Jackie said.'

She was backing away towards the bar, but one of Gerry's obnoxious friends put his arm around her and said, 'Give him a kiss then, love. He's getting married tomorrow. I think you should give him a kiss for a wedding present.'

'Yeah!' another piped up. 'How about that, Gerry? A kiss from a soap star. Wouldn't Sharon be mad if she knew?'

Thinking it best to go along with them, Lynne allowed herself to be pushed into Gerry's arms. He gave her a slobbery wet kiss and tried to put his hands down her blouse, making her flesh crawl. She was aware of a flash in the vicinity. Someone had taken a photo.

'Okay lads, that's enough!'

With relief Lynne heard Jim coming out from behind the bar, followed by Bob. They escorted her back to safety, while the men howled with rage at discovering their earlier quarry had escaped.

'I think you'd better just get your coat and leave, Lynne,' Bob advised her.

She didn't need any second bidding. Only when she was in her car did she realise how shaken she was, and for several minutes she just sat there with the motor running waiting until she was calm enough to drive home. If that was a taste of what fame could bring, heaven preserve her from it!

Next morning she rang her mother in Birmingham. Lynne's father had left them when she was fourteen and she'd never felt close to her mother since, but she felt she ought to tell her about her latest success.

Eileen Oakes listened to the news in silence then said, 'Oh well, I suppose your father would have been proud of you. It's the sort of thing that would appeal to him.'

Lynne felt bitterly hurt. She hadn't expected congratulations, but what she'd got was a metaphorical kick in the stomach. She had never forgiven her mother for allowing her father to vanish without trace. Although she'd made a few enquiries herself about Simon Oakes, the trail had gone cold and now, more than ever, she missed her dad's encouragement. If by some miracle he happened to see her on television and got in touch she would be overjoyed.

First, though, Lynne had to face herself on the screen. As the hour approached she poured herself a glass of wine and switched on the television. When the familiar theme tune began she found her hand was shaking as she raised the glass to her lips. She couldn't remember the last time she'd felt this nervous.

When the bar scene began it was quite a shock. Was that really her polishing glasses as she waited for Andrew to order his drink? She looked so . . . sexy. Under the studio lights her hair looked quite blonde, and her cleavage was accentuated. Then, when she spoke her first words, she was pleasantly surprised by how appropriate her voice sounded. It wasn't her normal speaking voice, but one she'd more or less unconsciously adopted for the part and it suited the character very well.

In fact, it would be obvious to anyone who knew her that she was merely acting. As relief swept over her, Lynne began to relax and even managed to enjoy her own performance. She noticed how quick Jonathan was to pick up his cues and give hers. He really was a good sort. Another actor might have tried to upstage her, but Jonathan was being very supportive and she felt grateful. By the time she saw her name on the closing credits she began to wish she'd invited some friends round – and cracked open a bottle of champagne to celebrate.

Then the phone rang. At once her jitters returned. Someone had seen her, formed an opinion, but who? Lynne hardly thought it would be her mother.

In fact, it was Nick. She was surprised at how much she enjoyed hearing his voice again. 'Lynne! I just switched on that soap thing, saw the last twenty minutes, and I couldn't believe it! But when I saw your name at the end I knew it had to be you. Fantastic! How on earth did you get the part? You were great!'

He hadn't sounded so enthusiastic for years. Suddenly Lynne felt truly proud of what she'd done. It was nice to be appreciated for a change, especially by the man she'd once loved.

They ended up talking for almost an hour. Finally, Nick said, 'Well, I suppose we should meet soon, to sort out the divorce arrangements.'

They had both agreed that there was no other way forward. Nick had left her for a woman at work called Jenny, and Lynne had bitterly resented his refusal to give her up. But he'd moved in with the woman ages ago, and her anger had faded somewhat. All she wanted now was to get the situation cleared up so they could both put their failed marriage behind them.

Lynne agreed to Nick calling round to see her the following afternoon. Before he arrived she changed her clothes several times and applied her make-up with more than usual care. She hesitated before spraying on any Dune, which had been his favourite perfume, but in the end she went ahead. The warm spicy-fruit aroma gave her the confidence she badly needed, because she had no idea how she would feel when she saw her husband for the first time in almost a year.

Nothing could have prepared her for the shock of seeing him again, however. It was obvious at once that she wasn't the only one who had changed. Nick had grown a beard, and his face looked altogether leaner and more handsome. His rather weak chin was now hidden, and his grey-blue eyes were subtly accentuated.

'Hello, Lynne. You're looking really good!' he began.

'So are you,' she smiled, and meant it. They were awkward with each other, trying to be polite, but the undercurrents were certainly there. Lynne thought she detected in Nick a shame-faced regret but also, she was surprised to find, a grudging admiration and attraction. Well, she thought as she led the way into the sitting room, if he reckoned I was going to sink into self-pity and depression forever he had another think coming!

Nick deliberately avoided the chair that had been his favourite, sitting instead on the sofa. He looked around, curious despite his obvious wariness. 'I see you've bought new curtains.'

'Yes, but we're not here to discuss the furnishings, are we?' Lynne snapped. She was suddenly irritated by the thought that he had developed his new image not for her, but for Jenny. The fact that it made him look far more attractive was doubly annoying.

Nick leaned forward with his elbows on his knees, his eyes gazing up at her appealingly. 'Look,

Lynne, this is no easier for me than it is for you, believe it or not. I still have mixed feelings about you. In fact, when I saw you on TV last night, I . . . oh well, never mind. The point is we shared five years together and some of that time was wonderful.'

'Yes, it was,' she said, ruefully. Seeing him now, after time had mellowed her pain, it was easier to remember the good times. 'Look, do you want a coffee or something?'

'That would be nice.'

He followed her into the kitchen and for a few seconds Lynne felt like bursting into tears. Somehow having him there in her kitchen again reminded her poignantly of the cosy domesticity they used to share. She filled the kettle, struggling to get a grip on herself.

'New fridge,' he commented.

'Yes. The old one conked out.'

'Already? That was a wedding present from my gran.'

'Well, I had a man look at it and he said it would cost more to repair than to buy a new one.' It dawned on her what a ridiculous conversation they were having. After throwing down the switch she snapped, 'Look, what I really want to know is, do I have to sell this house?'

He shrugged. 'That depends. Do you have the funds to buy me out?' Grimly, she shook her head. 'I thought so. Well, I suppose eventually it will have to be sold but I'm in no great hurry.'

'You've no plans to buy another house then, with Jenny?' It was hard to utter her name.

'No,' he mumbled, staring at his shoes.

'Okay. Well, I'd like to go on living here as long as

possible, then. The market's not too good at the moment, anyway. I doubt if we'd get more than eighty thousand.'

It was unreal, Lynne decided, discussing the state of the housing market in this detached way while all the time she had the feeling that neither of them wanted a divorce at all. Perhaps they should wait, but for what? It was all terribly confusing.

Back in the sitting-room, they drank coffee and talked about mutual acquaintances, all pretence at serious discussion ended for the moment. It wasn't long before Lynne became more relaxed, and even laughed at some of Nick's jokes. He'd been best man at the wedding of a mutual friend, and his account of the bridegroom's speech was hilarious.

'You mean, he actually said that about Diane's mum? I don't believe you!' she giggled.

'None of us could believe it. And the worse thing was, it was perfectly true!'

When her mirth had subsided she caught Nick regarding her thoughtfully. 'God, it's good to hear you laugh again, Lynne!' he murmured, coming over to stand beside her chair. 'It seems like years . . .'

'It *is* years,' she reminded him, soberly. 'Oh Nick, what went wrong? Do you know? Because I don't.'

'We were young, we had expectations,' he said simply. 'I thought you'd turn into a sweet little wife and mother, and you thought . . . I'm not sure. What did you want from me, Lynne?'

'I just wanted you to be happy, honestly, Nick. I'd have supported you in whatever you wanted to do, but I expected the same from you. When you talked me out of going to college I resented it like mad, and things went downhill from there.'

'Well you've certainly gone uphill again, Lynne. Maybe I've no right to say it, but I'm very proud of you, you know. I always knew you were special.'

He took her hand where it lay on the arm of the chair and kissed her fingers softly, one by one, the way he used to. Lynne felt a tremulous melting within, as if all her insides were gently dissolving and with them her resistance. Echoes of the desire she'd once felt for him were invading her consciousness, whispering wicked thoughts, willing him to follow through with more of the sweet attention he was giving her.

'Lynne?'

His unspoken question needed answering. She held her face up to him, open and vulnerable as her heart, and he bent to kiss her mouth. At first the unfamiliar roughness of his beard against her chin was disconcerting but she soon got to like it, relishing the reminder that he was undeniably a man. The softness of his lips was a contrast, her own lips yielding easily to the gentle pressure and allowing his tongue to enter.

He explored her mouth slowly, reviving memories of the bliss they'd shared when they were first together. She knew he was remembering all the secret places that turned her on, the crook of her elbow, the skin behind her ear, the soles of her feet. Beneath the pink cashmere sweater her breasts were straining against his chest, taut and demanding, while his fingers stroked her neck. Between her thighs she could feel her heedless pussy making ready, opening up for him, becoming slick with her juices.

Lynne told herself that they were still married and if he wanted her, she'd let him make love to her, show him what he'd been missing. She knew Nick was excited by her new, sexy image. He was sitting on the arm of her chair and she could feel the rigidity of his erection against her forearm. The thought of his penis, so sturdy and active when it was fully aroused, was creating a vortex of longing, making it impossible for her to resist.

Nick's hand began exploring beneath her jumper, feeling the rotund swell of her breast in its supportive bra cup. His thumb circled on her nipple, teasing it until the thin nylon covering was stretched to contain it, making sharp flashes of electricity shudder down her spine. Then he found the spot behind her ear and began to scratch it gently with his nails, filling her with excruciating desire. 'Oh God, Nick,' she murmured. 'What are we going to do?'

'What do you want to do?' he retorted, his voice thick with lust.

'You know what I want,' she gasped faintly as he swept her up into his arms and pulled her down on to the carpet. He grabbed a couple of cushions and put them under her, then, too impatient to undo the clasp, pulled the straps of her bra down as far as he could and plundered the full cups, groaning as his lips got their first taste of naked nipple.

Lynne knew that she wanted him to go all the way with her, to ease the frustration she'd felt after her encounters with Blake. She wanted cock, hot and ready, first for her fingers to stroke and her mouth to suck, and then to fill her completely. Her hands grabbed roughly at his fly and she pulled the zip halfway down before he realised what she was doing and completed the job. Never before had Lynne wanted anyone in this crude and almost violent way, but the sheer energy of it was incredibly exhilarating. While Nick pulled off her sweater and then found his way to the back of her bra, she delved into the front of his trousers and soon had his rampant penis in her hand.

It felt good to be holding his manhood once again, sliding her fingers up and down the solid length from the bulbous tip to the hairy root, then slipping under to feel his balls and cup their soft sac. Nick seemed equally content to play with her breasts, his hands following the heavy curves of her flesh with light, caressing strokes while he mouthed each of her nipples with delicate precision, sending her already fully activated nervous system into overdrive.

Soon Lynne was on her knees over him, letting her breasts dangle provocatively over his mouth while she struggled to free his penis from the last confines of his clothes. When he was naked from the waist down she lifted up his shirt and eagerly tongued the length of him, relishing the velvet texture of his shaft and the delicate salt taste at the tip. She took as much of his penis into her mouth as she could, feeling it lodge against the back of her throat, relaxing so that she wouldn't gag. She licked the underside with her tongue, making him groan his appreciation. He thrust impatiently and she began to rub the thick base, making him even bigger and lustier. Her empty vagina was crying out for him, and she knew that she couldn't bear to wait much longer and neither could he.

Nick's hands were working to undo her belt and soon his hand found its way into her pants, making her wetter than ever, making her want him badly. She lowered her breasts towards his willing mouth and he caught one of her nipples between his lips, pulling it out like rubber, making her shudder with the new sensations that swamped her awareness. Down below she could feel her clitoris huge and throbbing, responding despite his clumsy attempts to stimulate it with his fingers at an awkward angle, and she couldn't bear it.

Almost in desperation, Lynne pulled off what remained of her own clothes then mounted him, issuing a long sigh as she felt the hard member nose its way through the folds of her labia to find her entrance, then fill her with its solid length and girth. For a while she just let him stay there, safely docked, giving his shaft gentle squeezes with her vaginal walls, stimulating her clitoris indirectly and sending delightful ripples throughout her pelvic region. She looked down at him. He had both hands on her breasts now, his expression rapt, her nipples peaking through his outstretched fingers. Why on earth had they given up making love when it could be so good between them, so very, very good?

She didn't bother her head about it, but began to raise her hips in a slow and undulating rhythm that provided maximum stimulation where she needed it most. One of Nick's hands crept down from her breast and found her clitoris. His forefinger rubbed it gently from above, just the way she'd shown him all that time ago, and she was grateful that he was aiming to deliver her quickly from the throes of her frustration. Within a few seconds of him reaching her clitoris she felt the orgasm gathering force, focusing all her sensation on that one spot, taking her up and up towards the ultimate thrill while she rode him hard, hard, hard, wanting to take him with her.

And she succeeded. As the first climactic moments arrived for her Lynne could feel the hot pulsations coming from his penis as it thrust deep towards her shuddering womb. Together they rode the waves of each other's desire, urging each other on towards keener sensations and peaking in one glorious burst of wild fire from which they slowly descended in a warm haze. The gentle ripples went on and on, turning first into tremulous aftershocks then into echoes, until they finally petered out, leaving Lynne in a state of utter languor and sweet completion.

For a long time she lay motionless, her face sunk in the soft carpet, with Nick's arms around her and their twin heartbeats thudding in her ears. When she came to her senses a deep sadness overtook her and she began to sob uncontrollably.

'Don't!' she heard him say, kissing her neck and hugging her close. 'Please don't, Lynne.'

But she couldn't help herself. Their love-making had been so beautiful, and yet it was a sham. It was Jenny he loved, not her.

At the thought of the other woman all her old resentment returned and, suddenly, she got onto her knees and faced him, coldly. Steeling herself against his mildly perplexed smile and impossibly handsome face, she rocked back onto her heels.

'What I need is a bath,' she told him, with cruel indifference. 'Make yourself some more coffee if you like. We can talk later.'

She knew she was hurting him, but she didn't care. He'd hurt her once, irreparably, and this was small revenge. Leaping to her feet she hurried to the bathroom, locked the door behind her and started to run the water.

Once Lynne was lying in her scented bath she felt more relaxed – and guilty. She knew that she shouldn't have treated Nick like that, not after their wonderful love-making, but the pain of knowing she would have to say goodbye, to give him up again after all that unfettered passion, had been too great. She'd lashed out like a wounded animal, hoping to wound in return. She'd wanted to show him what he'd been missing, but had succeeded only in reminding herself that she was still alone. It was so unfair! He'd taken advantage of her vulnerability, acted on a whim of his own, and now he was back where he was while she . . .

The doorbell uttered its shrill call and she heard Nick shout from the hall to say, in the old, achingly familiar way, 'It's okay, Lynne, I'll get it.'

She glanced at her watch on the bathroom cabinet: half past five? It was an odd hour for someone to call, but maybe one of her friends had seen the programme and stopped by after shopping to congratulate her. Listening hard, she could make out Nick's voice and another man's, but that was all. Curious, she stepped out of the warm water and wrapped a towel around herself then went to the door, but by the time she opened it she heard the front door close.

'Who was it?' she called down to the hall.

Nick appeared at the foot of the stairs, bearing a huge mixed bouquet tied with a pink bow. 'Someone called Blake. He left you these.'

But Lynne was not looking at the flowers. She was staring down at Nick's thunderous face, and a spiteful urge to laugh took hold of her.

Chapter Four

'WELL, I SUPPOSE I'd better be going.' Nick turned from her with a sigh, his face strained, and Lynne felt awash with guilt. She shouldn't have smirked like that, not after she'd just made the most glorious love with her husband. It had begun to look like they might make a go of it after all, but Blake's untimely intervention seemed to have spoilt things between them.

'Look, that was just another actor from the show,' she told him placatingly. 'Blake plays Hugo – you know, the owner of the *Night Owls* club. I thought you'd have recognised him.'

'I don't care if he plays Donald Duck, he could still be screwing you!'

Lynne was taken aback by his anger. Once she would have been pleased that he was feeling what she'd once felt, but now she was merely sad. The worst of it was, she couldn't rebuff his taunt with any conviction. Okay, technically they hadn't screwed, but after their two torrid encounters it looked as if Blake wanted to continue their affair. Now she had impossibly mixed feelings about the two men in her life.

'I'm sorry, Nick, but obviously . . .'

'Obviously!' he snapped, pulling on his jacket. 'I'll be in touch, okay? We've still got stuff to sort out but I'm not in the mood right now.'

When he had left, Lynne tried to phone Blake but once again got his answerphone. She felt utterly confused about what she wanted. If there was a chance of making a go of it with another man she would be happy to divorce Nick and make a clean start. Yet she wasn't in love with Blake, and probably never would be, whereas she suspected that she was still in love with Nick, despite everything. But now he would go home to Jenny, thinking of his wife only in terms of dividing up possessions.

Lynne tried to put her personal problems on hold when she turned up at the studios on Monday. She was pleased to see that Blake was in that day and approached him as soon as she got the chance. 'Blake, I want to thank you for those lovely flowers,' she began brightly.

But when his world-weary eyes were turned on her they seemed cold and distant. 'Just my way of saying "congratulations" on your first TV appearance,' he said, unsmiling.

Lynne knew he must have jumped to conclusions about Nick. She began to explain, 'That man who opened the door . . .' then faltered, realising that nothing she could say would make it any better.

'Excuse me,' Blake said. He turned from her abruptly and greeted Sara Morton, who played Megan the nightclub singer, with a beaming smile. Lynne knew they'd had a well-publicised affair some time ago, and she felt a pang of jealousy. Now she had to fight against the resurgence of those feelings she'd had after the Rolls incident, which threatened her still-fragile self-esteem. Firmly she told herself that Blake's reaction wasn't entirely unexpected, and she couldn't allow herself to be fazed by it. There was work to be done.

After that shaky start, the day went well. This time Lynne really enjoyed her second scene with Jonathan. Andrew was supposed to have sobered up and had come to the bar to apologise for his girlfriend's behaviour. Carol had to say he shouldn't worry, it happened all the time when people had been drinking. She still had to act flirty with him, though.

'I thought you got the balance just right,' Jonathan said, during a coffee break. 'You're shaping up really well, Lynne.'

She was delighted. 'Thanks. That's the nicest thing anyone's said to me all day.'

'I couldn't help noticing that Blake seemed a bit off with you,' Jonathan continued tentatively. 'It's none of my business, but I thought you ought to know that he's a bit of a moody chap, and you shouldn't take it personally.'

'I'll remember that.'

'Don was furious when the story about him and Sara got splashed all over the front pages. He takes a dim view of that sort of thing. Mind you, others say it does the show some good, keeps us in the public eye. All I know is our ratings did go up while they were having an affair on screen and off.'

'I wonder what's in store for me then.' Lynne had meant to say, 'For Carol'.

'You won't know until the last minute,' Jonathan smiled, his blue eyes gleaming at her. 'They like to keep the storyline from us as long as possible, so there's less likelihood of a leak.'

'And I suppose that makes it more like real life, too.'

He gave her a rueful smile, that seemed to convey something more elusive, but then they were called back to the set.

Later, Lynne found herself wondering about Jonathan. He was being very nice to her, partly because they just happened to be thrown together by the dictates of the plot, but was there more to his interest than simple friendliness? He'd never mentioned a wife or girlfriend, and there was a definite attraction between them. At the moment, however, her life felt too complicated to take on a third lover. She'd been piqued by Blake's earlier treatment of her, yet she was still curious enough about him to want to see him again. There was a sense of unfinished business between them that she wanted to put right.

As for Nick, there was certainly unfinished business there. With a heavy heart she rang him that night, and was dismayed to hear his voice harden when she identified herself.

'Look, Nick, I think we should meet again fairly soon,' she continued staunchly. 'What about next weekend?'

'Maybe it should be on neutral ground. How about lunch at the Manor House?'

Lynne was surprised. He'd named a rather grand hotel in Richmond. 'Why there?'

'I want to check out their conference facilities.'

'Combining business with business, eh? All right. What time?'

'I'll meet you in the bar at half twelve.'

After she'd put the phone down, Lynne felt a

bleakness descend. She'd always felt that he had put his work before her, and he was still doing it. Well, if she got a free lunch out of it why should she complain?

While she waited for Nick to arrive on Saturday, surrounded by members of a wedding party, Lynne began to feel self-conscious. What if someone came up to her and said, 'Hey, haven't I seen you on television?' What on earth would she say? The thought of being asked for her autograph was quite daunting.

She told herself not to be so egotistical. It was unlikely that she would be recognised after only a couple of episodes. Besides, she was dressed more elegantly than Carol would ever be. After deciding to pull out all the stops for the occasion, Lynne was wearing her one tailored suit with a silk blouse. In fact she looked like a wedding guest herself, she noted wryly.

She must have blended in because Nick had difficulty finding her amongst the crowd. Seeing him arrive and scan the room nervously, Lynne enjoyed his mild anxiety.

'Oh Lynne, there you are!' he smiled at last, looking relieved. He was surveying her appreciatively as he walked towards her, and she knew just how he felt. She hadn't got used to his new look, either. In a smart suit and with his hair and beard tidily groomed, he had an air of suave sexuality about him that set her heart racing. Futilely, she reminded herself. Yet the attraction was still there, and she knew it was mutual.

'Sorry I'm a bit late. Do you want another drink, or shall we go and eat?' he asked, looking edgy. He'd never liked crowds, she remembered.

'Let's eat. I'm starving!'

Their conversation at the beginning of the meal was light and inconsequential, mainly about work. But then Lynne seized the opportunity to mention Blake.

'I thanked him for the flowers, but he was a bit short with me. Your opening the door to him must have put him off because he's been decidedly cool ever since.'

'I'm sorry. If I've ruined a budding romance, I mean.' Lynne thought she detected a smile of satisfaction lurking within Nick's beard.

'I was beginning to think that's what *we* had,' she said impulsively. 'Obviously I was wrong. But why did you lure me into sex, Nick? Just to prove you still could?'

He shook his head, vehemently. Then his eyes stared into hers with devastating effect. 'Don't think like that, please. I wanted to, that's all. And I believed you did too.'

'It was a spur of the moment thing,' she admitted. 'If I'd thought it through, I'd never have done it. I'm not into causing myself unnecessary suffering – I had enough of that while we were together. I'm getting my life back together now and I presume you are too. So maybe we'd better get this divorce sorted as soon as possible.'

'I suppose so.'

He looked downcast. Lynne reached out and put her hand over his. 'I'm sure it will be better in the long run. I'll be able to concentrate on my acting career, and you'll be able to marry Jenny, if that's what you want.'

'Ah! Well, that's what I'd intended to tell you. Jenny and I aren't living together any more.'

Lynne's heart gave an involuntary leap of excitement, even though she cautioned herself not to jump to conclusions. 'You mean, you've broken up?'

'Not entirely. We just needed a period apart to sort out our feelings. I'm still seeing her on a regular basis, but she's got a flat of her own. Jen felt we should wait till the divorce was over before getting back together permanently.'

Lynne steeled herself to ask, 'But you still love her?'

'After last weekend, I'm not sure. You know, Lynne, when that poor bastard appeared in your doorway I wanted to hit him! Then I realised there was still a lot going on between us, a closeness I couldn't deny. I was so miserable that weekend that I cancelled a date with Jenny, made some silly excuse. She's none too pleased, of course. She knew I'd gone to see you and now she's afraid we'll get back together again. And I'm finding it hard to reassure her because . . . well, damn it, half of me wants to!'

'Really?'

Lynne felt achingly hollow inside, unable to manage any more of the delicious salmon mousse that sat on her plate. She pushed it away, taking a sip of white wine instead.

Nick shrugged, looking equally disconcerted. 'I don't know. I'm still churned up about it.'

'Me too.'

For what seemed like a long time they sat in silence. Then their eyes met and Nick's were brimming over with frank appeal. He was waiting for a lead from her, but Lynne didn't know what to say. 'It's hard to talk here,' she said at last.

'We could always go for a walk in the park.'

'Yes, let's do that.'

Fifteen minutes later, when they were strolling in the boundless space of Richmond Park, Nick took her hand. 'Remember how we used to spend afternoons in the country, walking in woods?' he smiled. 'Especially at this time of year, when the leaves begin to colour. Trying to prolong the summer, I suppose.'

'Now we're just prolonging the agony!'

'Perhaps.' He stopped abruptly, beneath a vast spreading oak. 'Oh Lynne, I wish we could make a fresh start. Go back to the old days. Is it really impossible?'

She sighed, hope rising in her all the same. 'Things have changed. We've changed. I have my new career now, which means I wouldn't be so resentful of your work, but . . .'

Nick took her abruptly into his arms and began kissing her. She didn't resist. There was an inevitability about it, and she wanted him to know that his needs were hers, too. His tongue was as softly persuasive as his words, and now she felt the tide of her own desire rising, just as before. Leaning against the tree for support, Lynne could feel his thighs pressed against her, and a tremor of frustrated longing went through her.

'Oh, Nick – what can we do?' she moaned.

He stood back from her, looking dazed. 'I have to go back to the hotel,' he said, distantly. 'I haven't enquired about their conference facilities yet.'

Lynne felt squashed. She smoothed down her suit and turned away from him, bitterly disappointed. 'I see. I suppose I'd better get going then.'

'No, come back with me. Please?'

His eyes were full of naked appeal. 'All right. Maybe we should talk on the way.'

But instead of discussing divorce, Nick began opening up about Jenny as they walked back across the park, revealing things Lynne didn't particularly want to hear.

'I knew I'd made a mistake within a few weeks of going to live with her,' he confessed. 'But by then it was too late. My pride wouldn't let me go back.'

'I wouldn't have taken you back, anyway. Not then.'

'No, of course not.' He sounded miserable. 'But I did try to make a go of it with her. And I thought we were getting on okay, but she must have sensed that I hadn't got over you.'

Lynne didn't know what to say. She let him ramble on until the hotel came into view, then headed for the car park but Nick took her arm, restraining her. 'Look, let's have a drink or something. I don't want you to go yet. My business won't take long. You can wait in the bar.'

She agreed, despondently. After his revelations that afternoon she wasn't too keen on discussing how to split their CD collection, or divide the spoils they'd bought at car boot sales. All the same she didn't want to go home yet, just to spend the rest of the day feeling wretched.

Once Nick had seen the manager, they settled into a quiet corner of the bar. For some reason all he wanted to talk about was the past, their past, when things had seemed so much brighter. She was reminded of how happy they'd once been, before he'd wanted her to be a nice little company wife and she'd had other ideas. She was also reminded of how good the sex had been between them, and now Nick was making it obvious that he still wanted her. His eyes burned across the space between them, and he couldn't resist touching her hand, leaning close, breathing her perfume. Yet soon they would have to say goodbye to the past and look towards the future. Lynne found their conversation unbearably bitter-sweet as they reminisced about holidays they'd once enjoyed and old friends they'd now lost touch with.

'Look, Nick, I think I'd better go,' she told him, getting up. 'This is just depressing me.'

'Me too.' He followed her out into the foyer and she turned to say goodbye.

He gazed at her in desperation then, on impulse, took her hand. 'Shall we book a room?'

'What?'

'Here. Now. Just for a few hours.'

'Are you out of your mind?'

'Yes.' His simple affirmative stunned her. 'With desire for you, Lynne. Please, please don't deny me now.'

She couldn't believe her ears, and yet she so badly wanted to. He nodded towards the desk. 'They have spare rooms. I asked. Just in case.' Since she didn't answer he led her over to the receptionist and told the girl he would like to book a double room. Lynne was impressed. This was the old devil-may-care Nick in top form.

'How long for, sir?'

'Just for tonight. For me and my wife.'

Yes, Lynne thought, I still am his wife. It was so weird, booking in like any other married couple. Perhaps this was what they needed, a kind of impromptu second honeymoon. Now that she was used to the idea, letting him arrange it with a fatalistic kind of acceptance, she was looking forward to it. Relieved to be postponing the inevitable heartache a while longer.

'Room thirty-four,' Nick grinned at her, cheekily. 'We'll fetch the luggage later, shall we dear?'

Lynne nodded, still in a daze, and followed him to the lift. She felt as if she were in a nostalgic dream, re-living something they'd been through before, and when she glanced at his face it was almost like looking at a stranger. Exciting. She could feel her pulse racing, and the faint stirring of her libido. Were they going to make love again? Everything seemed to be pointing that way. As the lift stopped with a jolt she felt a keen thrill in her stomach, and knew that she wanted it as much as he did.

The room was large, with a king-sized double bed. Nick stood looking at her, his eyes examining her with searing intensity. 'God, I want you!' he growled, whipping off his tie.

Lynne carefully took off her clothes, hanging her suit in the wardrobe, until she stood before him wearing only her underclothes. Nick had removed all but his pants and shirt, which hung open to reveal his lightly-tanned chest and lean stomach.

'Come here!' he demanded brusquely.

She was happy to obey. By now her pulse was thudding in her ears and she could feel her body readying itself. Her nipples and clitoris were thrusting eagerly against their silken pouches, hungry for contact, and in between her longing was gathering strength, reaching out to all parts of her, making resistance impossible.

Lynne gasped as he pulled her close, forcing the air out of her lungs as his chest crushed her breasts and his lips descended on her still open mouth, his tongue plunging in at once to meet hers. While he kissed her, Nick led her to the bed and they sank on to it, arms and legs entwined, their bodies engaged in a heated exchange.

'God, how did we ever lose all this?' Nick muttered hoarsely, his hands almost squeezing her breasts out of her bra.

Lynne ground her throbbing mons against his thigh, wanting to ease the pain of her frustration. 'Carelessness?' came her wry reply. 'We must have been mad!'

'Crazy!' His lips travelled down to where he had managed to get one nipple free. 'Mm!'

The soft, wet contact of his mouth at her breast induced a sharp spasm of increased desire, deep inside her. She cried out, arching her back and thrusting her pelvis against him. Reaching behind her Lynne unclasped her bra with almost savage haste and struggled out of it, flinging it on to the floor.

Nick exclaimed with joy as her round, firm breasts were revealed to him. He seized one with both hands and pushed it up so that the nipple jutted towards his mouth, then he flicked his tongue lazily across it making Lynne groan with the impact of the heightened stimulation. She could feel herself soaking through the scrap of silk covering her vulva, and when at long last he freed one hand and let it wander down between her thighs, tickling her sensitised skin, she moved them apart hoping he would delve in between.

He found the wet cleft between her heavy, engorged labia and pushed his finger in. The silk clung to her like a second skin. Then he homed in on the protruding nub above, massaging it first with tentative strokes and then with increasing firmness until she was squirming helplessly, caught in the fierce pulsations that were leading her swiftly towards a climax.

Lynne felt the familiar buzzing warmth penetrate her to the core. Tense and expectant, she helped Nick to rid her of the last barrier of clothing and then sighed as his cool tongue found its way into her. His saliva felt like balm to her fevered flesh. She wriggled against him in sensual abandon, needing to continue the stimulation to her clitoris, welcoming back the pulsating joy of her swift ascent towards bliss.

When she was there at the threshold, hovering in sweet anticipation, Nick suddenly removed his mouth and left her stranded for a few seconds. She opened her eyes with a moan, but the sight of his full erection pointing between her legs was almost enough to trigger her. She felt another tremor pass through her, keen and abrupt.

Then, without preliminaries, he was right at the centre of her aroused sex, gasping with relief as his penis went in to the hilt. Lynne could feel him contained snugly within her walls while she waited for him to start moving. Where her clitoris was in contact with the thick base of his member she was on fire, throbbing with impatience, feeling the imminence of her climax and knowing that once the action began it would only be a matter of seconds before she came. Her hands passed rapidly down his smooth back to clutch at the hard buttocks, teasing her way down the deep cleft with a fingertip.

Nick levered himself up and began to rock slowly back and forth, first filling her completely and then, on the upward stroke, anointing her labia with her own juices. The sensations evoked by his leisurely movements were exquisitely subtle and when she was finally tipped over the brink the waves of pleasure came as soft internal caresses, infinitely delicate and sweet. Lynne wallowed in all the nuances of sensation as long as she could, hearing herself sigh in wonder as the ripples gradually died away.

'Oh, that was beautiful!' she breathed, still relishing the last tremulous whispers. Nick folded her into his arms and kissed her, then they dozed for a while.

It was his kiss that awakened her again, to memories of what they'd just shared, and she turned to him with a smile. 'I don't remember it being that good before. How about you?'

His smile turned mischievous. 'It's okay for some!'

'What do you mean?'

'Well it may have escaped your notice, but I've not actually come yet.'

'Oh!' She looked down the bed to where his erection was rearing boldly, the shiny head lifting itself from his belly in mute appeal, and smiled. Reaching down she sheathed the long shaft with her hands, and felt the solid flesh twitch in response to the warmth of her palms. Nick sighed and lay back, inviting her to do whatever she liked with him. And she did like. Bending her head to the enjoyable task she took the glans between her lips and tasted the salt bead that had gathered in the slit with the tip of her tongue.

Then, hungry for more of him, she let the whole of the tip enter her mouth, rolling her tongue around it while she gently manipulated the rest. His penis strained and grew larger, filling her mouth completely, and an answering twitch in her groin told her that soon she would want to envelop him with another part of her anatomy. She applied stronger pressure and the already hard flesh firmed up even more between her fingertips, while her lips moved with precision over the ridge at the top.

Nick suddenly sat up and grabbed her breasts. After putting her own desires on hold she felt them quicken as her nipples reacted with tingling urgency to his touch. She lifted her head and half turned, but he was too quick for her. Within seconds he had pulled her round, kneeling on all fours, so that he could enter her from behind.

Swiftly he slid into her well-lubricated vagina, making her gasp as he thrust against her raised buttocks, his hands catching hold of her breasts, weighing them in his palms and brushing his thumbs over the hard studs of her nipples. Lynne moaned her appreciation, remembering how much she'd loved this position in the old days, and began to buck her hips back and forth in rhythmic accord with his. One of his hands slipped down to her prominent clitoris to give her the extra stimulation she craved, and soon they were riding towards their mutual consummation.

As she felt him coming, in a wild burst of energy, Lynne's own climax began. This time the reverberations racked through her, turning her pussy into a throbbing centre of pleasure, making her cry out with the twin assault on her senses and emotions. Bitter-sweetness flooded through her, their erotic exchange both a joyful celebration of the love they had once shared, and a cause for regret that they'd let it slip away. As the physical feelings faded, Lynne was filled with determination that they should not lose something so precious again.

Nick, it seemed, had similar thoughts. As they lay in each other's arms once again, the heady smell of sex wafting around them like incense, he whispered into her ear, 'Lynne, I love you, and I always have. Do you think we could try again?'

'I don't know,' she sighed. 'But I'm willing to try if you are.'

'Shall we forget all this silly divorce stuff, then?'

Lynne saw no point in evading the issue. Least of all now, when they were open to each other. She'd been living on hopes and dreams as their marriage had crumbled around her, and had no intention of returning to that particular form of self-deception.

'What about Jenny?'

Nick's other woman had come between them, as tangibly as if she were lying there in the bed. Lynne felt his body grow tense. Then he turned, showing her the sadness in his eyes. 'I think it was over between us some time ago.'

'Are you quite sure?'

He said nothing, but his kiss said it all. I've won, Lynne thought triumphantly. I've got him back!

Chapter Five

LYNNE WAS LYING in bed on Sunday morning enjoying the peace and quiet. Beside her lay Nick, his hair dark against the pillow, his eyes closed, an expression of blissful relaxation on his face. Was he dreaming of her? She smiled to herself, but didn't attempt to wake him. He'd had a tough week at work and needed the rest.

Besides it was so good to lie there, relishing his presence. Although Nick had been living with her for three weeks she still hadn't begun to take their shared life for granted. Maybe she never would. Because Nick had changed since the early days of their marriage. He'd also had a 'makeover', since his body was now lean and taut from frequent visits to the gym, his hair and beard were subjected to more attention than when she first knew him, and his wardrobe had definitely improved. Never mind that his mistress had been the one responsible for those changes. His wife was now reaping the benefits, and she was not one to bear grudges.

Best of all, their sex life was absolutely fantastic! Lynne sighed and stretched voluptuously as she thought about last night's long session. It had begun with them both watching *Night Owls* in bed. Carol, Lynne's character, had been flirting with Hugo and had ended up kissing him in his office at the back of the club. The episode had ended on a cliff-hanger: was Hugo going to seduce her or not?

'What was it like, your first screen kiss?' Nick had asked her.

Lynne had done her best to describe the feelings of embarrassment, the fit of giggles that had to be got over, the way she had thought about Nick during the kiss itself to inflame her passion and make it look more realistic. What she hadn't told him was that she and Blake had a history. If he'd guessed, he chose to remain discreetly silent.

In fact the kiss had been very easy, given that it wasn't the first time she and Blake had embraced. Lynne had almost forgotten about the cameras and allowed their clinch to continue a fraction more than was really necessary. Jonathan had teased her about it, and she had the idea that he might have been slightly jealous. Still, she'd put the hurdle of her first love scene behind her now and it would never be so daunting again.

Nick sighed and turned in his sleep, flinging out his arm across Lynne's naked breast, making her flesh tingle delightfully. He'd given her three orgasms last night, with his mouth, his hand, and his prick. She'd been well satisfied. Yet afterwards, lying awake when he was already deep in slumber, she couldn't help wondering about his life with Jenny.

Although he'd never mentioned her, Lynne was sexually curious about the other woman. Had their love-making grown stale? It must have been good in the beginning, good enough for him to leave his wife. A stab of jealousy took Lynne by surprise and she mentally chided herself. What was she doing, spoiling their new love with pointless speculation? All that mattered was the present, and she was perfectly happy with it. Nick seemed even more so.

He stirred beside her, and this time she decided to respond. Kissing him on the mouth, she stroked his solid chest and shoulders until his eyes opened in faint surprise.

'Darling!' he murmured, sleepily, turning his hand over so that he could caress her already peaking breast. His fingers sought the nipple and rolled it slowly until she squirmed with pleasure. 'Mm! Last night was great.'

'Wasn't it just? Now do you want coffee right away, or shall we . . .'

He rolled on top of her, pinning her down with his strong legs and nuzzling her engorged breasts. He sucked on one ruddy, succulent nipple, making her hollow her back and grind her mons against his stomach, craving more stimulation. She burrowed into his hair with her fingers, making little groaning noises, feeling her growing desire for him course in heated paths throughout her body. Soon she was inflamed with new cravings, wanting him to touch her in different ways. She pushed him off her stomach and turned over, her arms above her head, pointing her buttocks towards him as a signal that she wanted him to touch them.

The warm feel of his palms on her behind was very arousing. Lynne inserted one hand down her front and found the hard bud of her clitoris, already slippery with her own juices. With a gasp of satisfaction she rubbed it with her forefinger and, at the same time, felt Nick run a finger down the cleft between her buttocks. He parted them and cool air fanned her exposed membranes, front and back. There was a pause while he dipped his finger in the pot of cream they'd used last night and which was still standing open on the bedside table.

Lynne raised her hips to allow him access with both hands. While she continued to rub herself in front, he slipped one finger into her willing pussy and the other into her anus, massaging them both gently. Lynne pressed herself further into the sheet, stimulating her breasts, then felt him kissing her neck behind her ear, which always made her come sooner.

The build-up to her climax promised to be short and sweet. Getting up on to her knees to give both her and Nick more room to manoeuvre, Lynne poked her behind provocatively into the air. She could feel her labia widening, exposing her inner lips, and her vagina stretched around his finger as if preparing to accommodate his penis. But that could wait. While Nick's double assault on her senses continued, she rubbed herself more speedily and strongly, just moments away from coming.

Then she stopped, pressing her hand against her mons to feel the hot throbbing, taking time to savour what Nick was doing. The cream had lubricated both orifices, letting his fingers slide easily in and out, in synch with each other. Lynne tightened both sets of muscles so that she could squeeze down on him during the outward strokes, refining her own sensations as she made minute circles with her wrist against her clitoris.

This time once the hot voluptuous waves began she didn't try to put on the brakes. Instead she went with the flow, revelling in the rush of energy that took her to her climax. She gasped as the spasms shook through her, time and again, stealing her mind and making her a total slave to her body.

Lynne still felt the after-shocks as Nick slowly withdrew his fingers from her and gently massaged her swollen labia. His strokings soothed her overheated flesh, helped her to come down from the violence of her orgasm and back to the lazy sensuality of its beginning. Soon she'd be ready to start all over again, but for now she was content to lie with one of Nick's hands sweeping over her buttocks and the other casually caressing her pussy.

His voice in her ear whispered, 'Coffee, madam?'

'Mm! Please.'

When he left her to go down to the kitchen, Lynne pulled the duvet up over her and lay enjoying what was left of her erotic glow. Although her climax had been supremely satisfying she still longed to feel his cock in her, wanted the feeling of being totally one with him, without boundaries, as if they were both immersed in the same warm bath.

Nick returned bearing coffee and orange juice. 'God, you look fantastic in this light,' he told her admiringly. 'I think you're even lovelier now than when I first knew you.'

'Thanks!' she grimaced, grabbing a glass of orange and drinking it down thirstily.

'It's wonderful falling in love with you all over again,' he continued, kissing her breast.

'That sounds like an advertisement for adultery,' she commented dryly.

'Oh, Lynne! Did you have to spoil it?'

Suddenly she felt riled. 'No, Nick, it was you who spoilt it, remember?'

'Are you going to spend the rest of our lives making me pay for it?'

He threw back the duvet, tried to turn her over and smack her behind, but she twisted away from him. Laughing, he lay beside her and took her into his arms. She snuggled close, but their earlier mood had changed to one of mild antagonism.

'Why her?' she asked at last. 'What was it about Jenny that attracted you to her?'

'Oh, I don't know.'

'Yes, you do. Tell me, I want to know. Is she pretty?'

'I suppose so.'

'Describe her.'

'Well, she has dark brown hair which she keeps long. And brown eyes to match.'

'Describe her body.'

Nick stared at her questioningly. Lynne was determined to pursue it. They had skirted the issue for too long and now she felt she had a right to know. 'Go on. Did she have nice tits?'

'Lynne!'

'I want to know more about this woman who took you from me.'

'Look, I understand how you feel, but I'd really rather not think about her any more. Not now I'm with you again.'

'But I need to know, to understand. Tell me what she had – or has – that I haven't got.'

'At the time she offered me enjoyable sex, I suppose. Without all the nonsense we seemed to go through. And she had a nice face and figure . . .'

'*Big* tits?'

'Biggish. Nice shape.'

'And she was good in bed?'

Nick turned away. Lynne knew she was going too far but she had to pursue it. 'Did you do things in bed that you hadn't done with me?'

'God, Lynne!'

'No, really. I want to know. Did she suck you off?'

'Sometimes.'

'Did she like anything kinky – bondage, or being whipped or anything?'

Nick made an exasperated noise and reached for his coffee. 'I think we should terminate this conversation right here. When I came up I was feeling really horny but now you've succeeded in putting me right off.'

Lynne snuggled up to his back, reached round and toyed with the tight curls of his pubic hair. 'But it's turning me on, Nick. The thought of you and her, I mean. I know I was your first real girlfriend, the first you'd fucked. I suppose you wanted to know what it was like with another woman, was that it?'

'Partly. But I'd never have strayed if things had still been good between us, you know.'

'They're good now though, aren't they? Better than it was with her?'

'I don't make comparisons. Jen was different, that's all.'

'Different? How?'

'She was more . . . difficult to arouse. Sometimes she didn't come for ages, sometimes not at all. But when she did it was all the more worthwhile.'

Lynne pondered this information. She supposed that Nick must have liked the challenge. Perhaps he'd had it too easy with her, since she'd always found it relatively easy to climax. Talking of which . . .

She finished her coffee quickly and got astride him. His penis was wilted now, but Lynne was confident that she could soon have it up and ready. Nick sighed, lying back and putting his arms above his head.

For a while Lynne avoided any direct stimulation of his member, preferring to kiss and stroke his strong, hairy thighs or run her hands lightly over his belly, making him convulse. When she finally bent her head it was to tongue his balls, licking them firmly as they moved around in their sac. As she did so Lynne lightly scratched the sensitive area between his scrotum and his anus with one fingernail, noting with pride that his penis was beginning to stir. She watched it writhe until it had re-oriented itself and was pointing up towards his navel but still she refrained from direct contact. His balls were heaving now, and his thighs moved restlessly against hers as she knelt over him.

Her hands began to make long sweeps up and down his body, brushing against his semi-erect organ in passing. Finally, when he was groaning at her to stop the torment, she took it between her palms and began to roll it, feeling the strengthening blood rush to fill its length, making the shiny pink bulb protrude from the darker sheath. Lynne gave the very tip an experimental lick, dipping into the slit. Then she applied her mouth in earnest, lips over the ridge between glans and shaft, tongue working secretly inside her mouth to bathe his most sensitive tissues with saliva. With finger and thumb around the base she could feel his erection growing by the second, making her own sheath, the one that ran deep inside her, wet with desire.

Feeling the need to stimulate herself further,

Lynne removed her mouth and inched further up the bed so that she could position his swollen tip within her labia. She held his penis just below the fleshy ridge and rubbed the glans gently up and down her slick folds, feeling her clitoris expand and throb with the more direct friction. She was hard too now, her tiny erection mimicking his.

Nick tried to push into her but she held back, keeping him where she wanted him, where she could gain maximum satisfaction for her sensation-hungry clitoris. He whimpered like a dog slavering for a biscuit. Lynne relented a little, letting the head of his prick dock briefly in the outer ring of her vagina and squeezing a few times. But then she brought it out and stroked her vulva with it, relishing the renewed lubrication of her tumid lips. It pleased her to be denying him and pleasuring herself. The tiny knot of anger over his infidelity was still there in the murky heart of her, tingeing her lust with vengefulness. She would make him wait for it this time, damn him!

Meanwhile, she was enjoying herself to the full. The solid column of flesh in her hand was an excellent tool for rubbing her clitoris – almost as good as an electric vibrator. Ignoring Nick's protests she began to increase the pace, jiggling her hips at the same time, drawing herself towards a climax with rapid strokes. Lynne could feel her breasts shuddering heavily as she rocked up and down, her buttocks slapping rhythmically against his thighs. She was so hot and slippery down there that once or twice she let his dick slot into her by mistake but immediately pulled it out again and continued her self-stimulation.

She was panting now and sweating with her

exertion, very near to orgasm. Nick was almost howling with frustration as his prick continued to be used as a clit-stimulator, keeping him so frustratingly from his goal. Then, when Lynne recognised the first thrilling moments of her climax, she knew she wanted him inside her, to make her satisfaction complete. Deftly she pushed him back down and straight into her vagina, letting him feel the shock waves engulf him as he sank into her with a loud groan.

The relief of having something to clutch at, something solid for her pussy to feel, made Lynne's pleasure more acute. She knew Nick had started to come almost as soon as she let him in, but her inner walls continued working of their own accord, pumping him furiously as her own orgasmic experience overwhelmed his. Long after he'd finished she was still buzzing with energy. She felt him droop inside her and slide out, but then she pressed her thighs tightly together and the thrilling feelings were prolonged for a few, precious seconds more.

At last she fell back exhausted onto the pillow. Turning to Nick, she tried to cuddle up to him but he moved away from her and left the bed saying, 'I think I'll take a shower.'

He was gone before she knew it, leaving Lynne faintly worried. Had she overstepped the mark in putting her satisfaction before his? Surely she was entitled to be selfish in bed, once in a while? Besides, there would be plenty of opportunity to redress the balance another time.

As the leisurely day unfolded, Lynne was reassured by her husband's calm, contented manner. When bedtime came round again, however, she detected a new mood of defiance in him. 'You had your wicked way with me this morning,' he told her, as they brushed their teeth together. 'But tonight it's my turn, okay?'

'Of course. Fair's fair!'

'I can have you any way I want you?'

'Within reason.'

'Right. When you're through here, come downstairs wearing your science overall and that sexy underwear you once tried to tempt me with.'

'My *science* overall? You mean, my school one?'

'You do still have it?'

'Yes, it's in the wardrobe. But . . .'

'Never mind. Put on that black underwear you got from the catalogue, and then the overall. Leave the top buttons undone to show your cleavage. I'll be in the front room.'

Intrigued, Lynne fetched the half-cup bra and open-crotched panties from her underwear drawer. Last time she'd worn those it had been for Blake. She suspected that this time would be more fun.

Dressed as Nick had directed, and smelling of Dior's 'Tendre Poison', Lynne crept downstairs. The door to the living room was shut. She knocked and was told to 'come in'. Nick was sitting there wearing only his shirt and underpants.

'I got undressed, Nurse, just as you said,' he began nervously. 'But I've never been to the sperm bank before. What do I have to do?'

Lynne repressed a smile. So that was his game! A frown passed fleetingly over her brow as she wondered whether playing sex-games had been Jenny's secret weapon. But then she thought how appropriate it was for her. After all, she was supposed to be an actress now!

'Well, Mr Smith, it's quite simple really. We need

a sample of your sperm to go into this receptacle.' Improvising, she seized a glass ash-tray from the coffee table.

'And how do I do that?'

'The usual method. Would you rather I left you alone? We did have some magazines that you might have found useful, but they seem to have disappeared.'

'Oh.' Nick looked up at her with pleading eyes. 'I think I'm going to find it rather difficult, then. Would you . . . could you . . . I mean, I could do with some help.'

'I see.' Lynne paused for thought. She decided to prolong the agony a little. 'Isn't there someone you could, you know, think about? Kim Basinger, for instance. Most men seem to find her sexy.'

'She's not as sexy as you, though.'

Lynne pretended to be shocked. 'Really, Mr Smith!'

'Perhaps you could just undo another button on your overall, Nurse. You see, I don't even have an erection yet and I think I'm going to need quite a lot of stimulation before I get going.'

'Oh dear! Perhaps just one button, then.'

When Lynne undid the third button her front gaped considerably, since the fourth button was missing. Nick gasped with unfeigned delight as her entire cleavage was revealed.

'Oh, that's much better! I can feel things starting to happen already.'

'You can see so much of me there's no point in keeping this on now, is there?' Slowly Lynne removed her overall to reveal her scantily clad figure. Nick pulled off his pants and the full extent of his erection appeared beneath his shirt. It was impressive.

'Who's a big boy, then?' Lynne cooed. 'Do you want me to stand here while you do it?'

'Yes, that should help. Or maybe you could hold the receptacle for me.'

'Good idea!'

Lynne came to kneel before him, holding up the ash-tray. She felt absurd, but also very aroused. It wasn't like doing the soap. There was a complicity between them that was extremely exciting. She had an idea where the scenario was leading, but she didn't know exactly, and that was half the fun.

Nick began to pull at his extended penis, then to rub it more forcefully. He was staring at her semi-naked breasts and she could feel them tingling under his intent gaze. Then, quite suddenly, he stopped. 'I'm afraid it's no good, I just can't seem to come.'

'Is there some other way I can help you?'

'You could let me do it between your tits. I'm sure that would work.'

'All right, then. It's in a good cause, after all. Do you want my bra on or off?'

'On, I think.'

'Good. Come on then, let me help you.'

Lynne shuffled forward on her knees, reaching out for his firm penis and placed it in her cleavage. It felt warm and smooth, titillating the responsive skin of her breasts. She could feel her nipples tingling deliciously, only just out of reach of his thrusting organ.

'Shall I stroke your balls?' she asked him.

He nodded. 'Yes, please. May I stroke you at the same time – down there?'

She guided his hand down between her thighs where her pussy was already soft and wet. He gasped with pretended surprise as his fingers found access straight away.

'Rude knickers!' he commented.

'Oh, yes! My husband loves me to be opened up for him at any time of the day or night.'

'He doesn't mind you working in a sperm bank, then?'

'Oh no, he loves it! Says it reminds me of sex all the time, so I'm good and ready for him when I come home.'

Nick was stroking her labia now with gentle fingers, while she held his cock and worked it back and forth in her cleavage. A thin film of semen was making her breasts feel sticky and she knew it wouldn't be long before they achieved their objective. Her own longing was growing too, the physical stimulation combining with the mental to turn her on very rapidly.

Suddenly he spurted, in a series of shuddering emissions that happened far too quickly for Lynne to make any pretence at capturing the semen. Nick fell back groaning and, when he had recovered slightly, commented, 'Oh dear! I'm afraid I couldn't control myself.'

'Never mind,' Lynne smiled, sweetly, wiping her chest with a towel conveniently to hand. 'We can always try again when you feel up to it.'

But then, to her alarm, he sprang to his feet, dressed hurriedly and dashed from the room. He entered again at once, this time with an expression of horror on his face.

'Nurse Wilkins! What is this I hear about you lewdly assisting the young men who come here in good faith to give their services? I cannot believe . . . Oh, my goodness! I'm afraid I have to believe it now, seeing you in that disgusting state. What a wanton slut you are! You're a disgrace to the nursing profession!'

Lynne did her best to appear contrite. 'I am sorry, sir. You see, the young man in question was having some trouble producing the required specimen. He asked me to give him some assistance.'

'And you found it necessary to wear such revealing and immodest underwear? Really, Mrs Wilkins, I cannot allow such blatant impropriety. I'm afraid I shall have to dismiss you.'

Beginning to guess at what Nick wanted, Lynne threw herself at his feet. 'Oh no, please, sir! Don't give me the sack! It's so hard to get jobs these days, and we depend on my salary.'

'You should have thought of that before you behaved so improperly. But perhaps if you were to submit to some form of punishment, I could let you off this time.'

'Punishment, sir?'

'Yes. I am a great believer in the old-fashioned remedy of corporal punishment, particularly for sins of the flesh. Would you be willing to undergo a spanking, Mrs Wilkins?'

Lynne looked suitably shame-faced. 'I suppose so. Would you administer the punishment yourself, sir?'

'Of course, and as speedily as possible. If you would care to bend over my lap while I sit in this chair I shall give you a dozen slaps with my bare hand. I consider that to be an appropriate penalty and a deterrent against future misdemeanour.'

'Yes, sir. Thank you, sir.'

'You should not thank me until we are both satisfied, Mrs Wilkins.' Nick plonked himself down in the arm chair with his legs apart. Lynne noticed that his fly was undone and the bulge of his erection could be seen beneath his white pants. 'Now, place yourself across my thighs.'

Lynne bent over him, pushing her bottom high in the air. The black panties consisted of little more than a lace string around her hips and a thong between her buttocks, so that she was revealing her buttocks in their entirety. While she grasped the arm of the chair with one hand to support herself, she slyly placed her other hand very near to the pouch that contained his penis.

'Are you ready, Nurse?' Lynne nodded. 'Then brace yourself!'

The first slap was quite mild, stinging her only momentarily on the right buttock. The second came down with equal restraint on her left. Lynne could feel her flesh quiver under the impact of the blows, and as the beating proceeded a not unpleasant warmth spread slowly through her lower region from back to front, exciting her. She shifted position slightly and took the opportunity to place her hand right over her husband's cock. When he next raised his arm to deliver the final blows she could feel him grow stiff beneath her hand, and knew that he was enjoying their play-acting as much as she was.

Nick brought his hand down with greater force as the thrashing neared its climax and Lynne felt her clitoris throbbing hotly as she wriggled about in his lap. Surely he wasn't going to leave her unfulfilled after this wonderfully arousing session? That would be punishment indeed. Slowly she got to her feet and stood with head bowed, awaiting further cues.

'I hope you are grateful to me for that,' she heard him say.

'Oh yes, sir. Thank you, sir!'

'But we are one donation short today, since you so wickedly wasted that young man's contribution. Perhaps you would take mine instead.'

Lynne brightened. This was more promising. 'Oh yes, certainly, sir!'

She reached for the ash-tray, but he took it from her. 'You won't be needing that. You will be collecting my specimen in your own personal receptacle. Lie on the floor now, Mrs Wilkins, with your knees bent wide apart. I wish to examine you.'

She saw him pull off his pants and discard them, his penis rearing with lusty enthusiasm under his shirt, which he kept on. Then he knelt down and peered at her between the frilly edges of her panties. 'Hm! I suppose this form of underwear has its uses. You look very healthy down there, Mrs Wilkins, but I need to make an internal examination. Lie still, now.'

His fingers were soft and gentle, sliding easily inside her and making her sigh with voluptuous contentment. She was all liquid inside, and in a moment he would be giving her what she wanted, what they both wanted. His hands slid beneath her buttocks, lifting her a little and cushioning her against the roughness of the carpet. Then he knelt and pushed into her with his prick. She could tell it was a fine erection, filling her completely as he thrust forward, making her gasp with the sudden sweetness that flooded through her.

Unable to resist her provocatively exposed breasts, he took one of her hardened nipples in his mouth and sucked it while he fingered the other one. Lynne found herself making involuntary movements with her pelvis as the pace quickened, wanting him so badly, needing that ultimate thrill towards which his rapid movements were propelling her. Nick was red-faced with exertion now, hammering at her as if their intercourse was truly a continuation of her punishment. Fearing that he might come before she did, Lynne ground her mons against him in her frantic attempts to push herself over the edge.

With shattering fierceness the first convulsions of her climax had her bucking and moaning, triggering Nick in their wake. Needing some way to express the overflow of energy that she couldn't contain, Lynne beat on the floor with her fists and heard herself shout out loud. The orgasm was violent in its intensity, and left her utterly spent.

Lynne flopped back, collapsing into complete inertia. She was aware of Nick coming out of her and moving away, covering her with something warm and cosy. Then she drifted off.

When she awoke Nick was sitting in the armchair nearby, sipping whisky. He smiled down at her. 'Welcome back, darling! Would you like a drink?'

'Mm. Something long and cold. I'm parched!'

Lynne felt better once she had more liquid inside her. She put on the dressing gown that Nick had brought down and cuddled up in the chair with him.

'So, what's the verdict?' he asked eventually. 'Did you enjoy that?'

'Yes.'

'You sound a bit doubtful.'

'Well, I'm not sure I want to go through all that every time. It was fun, but quite tiring.'

Nick smiled, his blue eyes regarding her fondly. 'Special occasions only then, eh?'

'All right.'

Lynne fell silent, wondering how often he'd played those games before. If only she could get Jenny out of her mind, but it was asking the impossible. No matter how wonderful the sex, how close she felt to Nick, that invisible third party would remain, hovering in the shadowy borderlands of her consciousness. Would she ever manage to exorcise that woman's ghost?

Chapter Six

'DID YOU SEE "Soaplines" this week?' Jonathan had a copy in his hand as they stood in the coffee bar at Sphere TV. Lynne looked at the magazine, shaking her head. His grin widened. 'Just take a look – top of page two.'

She saw the headline: SOAP BARMAID IN REAL-LIFE PUB CLINCH! With a sinking heart Lynne recognised herself in the Red Lion, but she wasn't serving behind the bar. Some strange bloke had his arms around her and was giving her a passionate kiss. Anger welled up in her, overcoming the initial shock of embarrassment. What the hell was going on?

Then she remembered. That stupid stag night! There had been a flash as she'd let herself be kissed by the bridegroom, but she hadn't taken much notice at the time. Obviously someone had decided there would be a few quid in it for them if they sold it to that rag.

'God, how sickening! It didn't mean anything, Jonathan. Some lads got drunk and a bit rough, so I agreed to kiss that guy just to defuse the situation.

Now they've blown it out of all proportion.'

She read on. 'Who is the mystery man kissing sexy *Night Owls* barmaid Carol? Not actress LYN SANDERS' husband, that's for sure! Electrician MICK SANDERS was conspicuous by his absence on the night in question. Obviously luscious Lyn can pull more than pints – she can pull the lads as well!'

Lynne tossed the magazine back at him in disgust. 'Not only is it making something out of nothing, but they've spelt my name wrong! And they've called Nick 'Mick'. And he's not an electrician, he's with an electronics firm. God, doesn't it make you sick!'

Jonathan smiled ruefully. 'It's the way of the world, Lynne. We all have to put up with it. But no-one takes showbiz gossip seriously. They'd go mad if they did!'

'I thought you said Don didn't like us getting publicity.'

'I think he's resigned to it now. He gave Blake a dressing-down once, but then the scriptwriters altered Hugo's character, making him more of a ladies' man. A case of art mimicking life, I suppose.'

'Well I hope they don't turn Carol into an out-and-out tart, that's all!'

Lynne decided she was not going to buy 'Soap-lines'. When she got home, however, she was shocked to see a copy lying on the coffee table. Nick confronted her with it at once.

'Have you seen this?' he snapped, his face distorted with rage.

Lynne took a deep breath. 'Yes, they showed me at the studio. I'm really sorry, Nick. It was just a prank. I had no idea I was going to end up in there.'

'Prank? God, Lynne, what on earth were you up to?'

She told him the full story, ending with, 'If you doubt my word you can ring Jackie. Or Bob, the barman. They'll tell you exactly what happened.'

'That's not the point. The harm's already done.'

She wasn't used to seeing him furious. It brought back memories of his opposition to her plans to return to college, and she didn't like it. Now, though, she knew of a sure way to deflect his anger. Putting on a contrite face, she suggested, 'I know I've been a naughty girl, Nick darling, and I deserve punishment. Shall we go upstairs? Then you can teach me a lesson I won't forget!'

A slow smile spread across her husband's face and, with a secret flash of triumph, Lynne knew she'd won.

In the bedroom, she awaited his orders. 'This is more than a minor misdemeanour,' he declared, frowning. 'So I think it requires more than a few taps. Strip to your underwear, woman!'

Meekly, Lynne obeyed. As she stood there before him in her bra and pants she felt a wild thrill of expectation shudder through her. What did he have in mind? Since Nick had given her that first spanking she'd often fantasised about receiving another, although the occasion hadn't presented itself until now.

There was a brass rail at the head of their bed, and as he approached with a length of cord in his hand Lynne knew that she was going to be tied to it. She pretended to be dismayed but he threw her, face down, on to the bed and tied her wrists to the rail.

'Now I've got you where I want you, vixen!' he snarled.

'You beast!' she moaned. 'What are you going to do to me?'

'Wait and see.'

Lynne heard him take off his clothes then go to the wardrobe and take something out. Craning her neck round she caught sight of him in the mirror, with a feather duster in one hand and a giant erection in the other. The incongruous sight made her giggle, but she was aroused all the same. Her bra was riding up due to the extension of her arms and her breasts were bulging beneath their cups. Although her legs were free, she couldn't kick or wriggle too much because it put too much of a strain on her shoulders. The feeling of being constricted was oddly exciting, making her clitoris tingle as she ground it ineffectually against the bedclothes.

'Now, Miss Demeanour, prepare to atone for your sins!' she heard her husband say. 'Kissing another man in public is a very serious crime, but being photographed and splashed all over the pages of a scurrilous magazine compounds the offence disgracefully.'

All the while he was speaking, Nick was delicately tickling her exposed buttocks with the clump of feathers. Lynne was soon writhing voluptuously, especially when he probed gently between her spread thighs and into the damp folds of her labia. Soon she was letting out involuntary moans of desire.

But then, quite suddenly, she felt the other end of the implement come down hard upon her naked behind. Nick had whacked the wooden handle right across both buttocks, making her gasp. She could feel her skin smarting horribly, but then he changed ends and resumed his feathering of her skin so that she began to be soothed again. No sooner had her flesh become used to the gentler treatment than he delivered another stinging blow, followed by more feather-light touches. The combined effect of this was very stimulating, and Lynne felt herself becoming wetter and wetter with each blow.

The alternate thrashing and caressing went on until she'd received twelve strokes, then she heard him throw the duster to the floor. Unsure what would happen next, she lay in trembling suspense until she heard him clamber on to the bed behind her. Then, without any preliminaries, he grabbed her breasts and pushed his penis into her from behind.

'Slut,' he snarled into her ear, as he began to thrust with a vigour that soon had her panting. 'Promiscuous slut! Disgusting little whore!'

Lynne had never heard anyone talk to her like that. At first it was unreal, as if she were acting her rôle in *Night Owls*, but after a while she found the combination of his aggressive words and equally forceful actions very stimulating. Her tumid labia were being worked hard and fast, back and forth over her pulsating clitoris. The sensations were intensifying, dulling her mind and sharpening her senses so that she became almost mechanical in her movements and responses, her inner walls embracing the beloved invader, bringing her close to a climax.

Before she could get there, though, Nick exploded. Lynne could feel him pumping into her, but no matter how hard she squeezed him her own satisfaction remained elusive. With a groan he pulled out of her and slapped her tender rump, making her wince. Then he reached up and untied the cord that bound her to the rail, freeing her aching wrists.

Lynne, still on her knees, looked down at him. He lay beside her, utterly spent. 'I'm not finished yet,' she told him. 'I haven't come.'

His blue-grey eyes looked up at her and he grinned slyly. 'All part of the punishment.'

'What?'

He dodged out of the way of her fists and got to his feet. 'You heard.'

'Get out of here, Nicholas Sanders!'

He obeyed, chuckling, and for a while she lay in a daze until she became aware of the raw energy still humming away within her. Casually her hand drifted down until she touched the enlarged bud of her sex. It responded at once to her fingertip and she began to rub more vigorously, welcoming the return of her former arousal now that it was in her power to satisfy herself. With her other hand she felt the moistness inside, pushing right in so that she could feel through the wall to the very root of her throbbing clitoris. The twin approach soon had her rolling on the bed in heedless ecstasy, her breasts thrusting towards the ceiling as she moved this way and that, desperate to finish what had been left undone by her husband.

With a loud groan of relief Lynne gave herself up to the final thrilling moments, squeezing down on her fingers to wrest every last second of pleasure from the experience. When it was over she was conscious of the tenderness of her behind and remembered its cause with a wry smile. Had it settled the score between her and Nick? She did hope so.

For a while everything seemed fine, and Nick didn't refer to the incident again despite the fact that some of the lads at work gave him some stick over it.

But a week later Lynne returned from the studios to find him in a black mood.

'Some bloody reporter showed up on the doorstep,' he told her as soon as she entered the house. 'Wanted to know if Lynne Sanders lived here. I told him to sod off.'

'Oh dear!' Lynne was genuinely upset. 'Where was he from, do you know?'

'Local rag. Followed up the story, I suppose. Once those devils get the scent they won't leave you alone.'

'Maybe you scared him off,' she suggested, but without much conviction.

Half an hour later, the phone rang. 'Is that Lynne Sanders?'

'Speaking,' she replied automatically.

'This is Dan Fielding, from the *Echo*. I was wondering what you thought of being featured in "Soapline" magazine?'

'What I think is unprintable!' she snapped.

'So you're none too pleased. But what does your husband think about it?'

'He's furious too. Not least because of people like you turning up on the doorstep.'

Nick had come to the phone. 'Who is it, Lynne?'

She put her hand over the receiver. 'Reporter. From the *Echo*.'

To her surprise, Nick snatched the phone away from her and replaced it. 'You fool! Don't you know that anything you say will be taken down and used in evidence?'

'Evidence of what?'

'Of anything they want people to believe. They'll blow it up out of all proportion now. The only way to deal with those bastards is to say nothing at all.'

He turned out to be right. The next edition of the local paper bore the headline: 'SOAP BARMAID'S CANDID CAMERA KISS'. The article amazed Lynne. Somehow the reporter had managed to make a news story out of minimal information: 'Soap star Lynne Sanders ('Carol' in *Night Owls*) was hopping mad when she saw a photo of herself kissing bridegroom-to-be Gerry Porter in the latest edition of "Soap-lines". The real-life clinch took place at Gerry's stag night at the Red Lion, where Lynne used to work behind the bar. His bride-to-be, Sharon Brown, said she nearly divorced him when she saw it. The Red Lion's landlady, Jackie Carson, confirmed that the ex-barmaid did it "for a lark" but husband Nick was not so sure. Lynne admitted he was furious at his wife's antics, and her own opinion of the scurrilous soap mag was said to be "unprintable". Well, Lynne, we've got news for you: what you do on screen is one thing, but when soap stars behave like that in their own local, folk get into a real lather!'

'I hope you're satisfied!' Nick growled, throwing the paper down in disgust.

Lynne tried to put her arms round him but he pushed her away. 'Look, love, I'm truly sorry. I'll be more careful in future, I promise.'

This time there was to be no therapeutic rôle-play to get her off the hook. When they went to bed that night Nick treated her roughly, pinching her nipples cruelly and thrusting into her before she was ready so that she ached with the pounding. Afterwards she felt used, and told him so. 'I'd rather not make love at all than like that.'

His eyes glittered harshly at her in the dim light. 'You deserved it.'

'I did not! How dare you say that?'

'I won't have my house invaded by the press, Lynne.'

'But that's no reason to take it out on me physically.' She stared at him, wondering what had happened to the Nick she once knew. Had he really changed that much? A dull disappointment was beginning to fester in her after the joyful start to their reunion.

Next day Lynne was kept busy at the studio. Carol was to appear on a different set from the usual club bar, visiting Andrew's girlfriend at her flat. The idea was that she should try to make Penny understand that there was nothing going on between her and Andrew. However, she lost her bottle when she found he was there, made her excuses and left in a hurry.

When Lynne returned home she found Nick in a bad mood again and her heart sank. 'Your mother phoned,' he told her sourly. 'She had that article shown to her by someone at work, and she wasn't pleased. She wants you to ring her.'

Lynne felt saddened, and exasperated. She had just about managed to convince her mother that she and Nick were truly reconciled. Now, as she answered her call, she guessed that she was in for another dose of 'I told you so'.

'Really, Lynne, I thought your being in that vulgar soap opera was bad enough!' came Eileen Oakes' shrill tone, before she could get a word in. 'But to find my daughter plastered all over the pages of a scandal magazine was the last straw! Have you no dignity? And what does poor Nick think about it? I should think he's horribly upset. After he'd agreed to come back to you, as well. I suppose he'll be leaving you again now, and I wouldn't blame him. I knew it couldn't last.'

She let the harsh voice rant on, since there seemed to be no point in trying to justify herself. The worst of it was, her mother had expressed her own fears. What if Nick did leave her again?

Lynne tried very hard over the next few days, cooking Nick delicious meals and doing her best to seduce him when they went to bed. Remembering how well he'd responded to her wearing a white coat, she invented a new game on her way home from work and tried it out on him one night. While he was downstairs watching television she dressed herself in her overall again, this time with nothing on underneath, then ran a bath. Returning downstairs, she knocked on the closed door of the sitting-room calling, 'Your bath is ready, sir!'

'What?' she heard him turn off the TV set and come to the door, flinging it open. He looked startled and, for a moment, Lynne was afraid he wasn't going to play the game. She smiled, repeating, 'I've run your bath for you, sir. It's nice and hot.'

'My bath, Nurse? Suppose I'd better have it, then.'

He'd fallen into the rôle at once, putting on a grumpy tone as if he were an elderly invalid. Lynne took him by the arm and 'helped' him upstairs, making sure her body was pressed close to his and that her overall revealed plenty of naked thigh. Once in the bathroom, she undressed him carefully then supported him as he stepped into the steaming water. As she leaned over the edge of the bath much of her cleavage was visible.

'Now just you lie back and let me soap you all over,' she said in a businesslike voice.

Lynne had chosen a luxurious new bar of soap that lathered profusely. She began to enjoy the creamy silkiness of it on her hands as she smoothed it over his back and shoulders. Imagining what it would feel like on her breasts, she felt her nipples harden beneath the stiff white cotton of her overall. 'Now your arms please, sir.'

He flung one hand out and groped between her breasts. At once she slapped his wrist. 'Naughty! They're not for the likes of you.'

'Spoilsport!' he whined, ogling her cleavage.

She made him kneel on all fours while she washed his bottom, letting her finger stray and making him moan with pleasure. Then she reached down and washed his balls, relishing their slippery smoothness. Deftly she reached behind them and caught hold of his warm penis, which she proceeded to soap thoroughly. His low moaning reached a crescendo and she felt his erection grow in her hand.

'Lie down in the water again, you dirty old devil, and wash it all off!' she ordered him.

He gave her a sheepish look. When he sank back into the water his prick stood up like a periscope and it was all she could do to keep from giggling. Instead she told him, 'All right, now we'll have you out of there.'

Wrapping him in a large bath towel Lynne led him through to the bedroom, where she had him lie face down on the bed. 'I'm going to give you a nice rub down with this special cream. It will be good for your rheumatics.'

The body cream was thick and soft as butter, and smelt of jasmine. As Lynne began to cover his back with it she revelled in the sensual scent and feel, hoping that later Nick would return the favour. Already she could feel her labia swelling between her thighs, the pulse throbbing in her sex. She ran her sticky palms over his pink buttocks, feeling the muscle beneath, and then down his hard legs.

'All right, now you can turn over.'

Predictably his penis was still erect, pointing straight up near his navel. Lynne ignored it at first, concentrating on rubbing the cream into his well-moulded chest. The tiny nipples quickly became hard as she brushed her palms across them. She could see Nick staring at her breasts, and knew that the outline of her own nipples could be clearly seen beneath the rough cotton, as hard as his and four times the size. A small shudder went through her as she imagined him doing to her what she was doing to him.

Starting at his feet she made her way slowly up his shins and thighs, rubbing the cream in well. 'Oh, that feels good, Nurse!' he said in his old man's voice.

She smiled. 'The best is yet to come. Lie still and let me do it all, there's a good chap.'

Soon she was circling round his belly, avoiding his rampant penis until she had him groaning with frustration. 'Finish me off quick, Nurse!' he begged, but still she took her time.

Then, when she finally took the straining member in hand, he let out a loud groan. Lynne soon made it slippery, enjoying the way it slid under her firm control, feeling the hard rigidity beneath the viscous surface. She rolled and tugged at him with alternate hands until she felt the first pulsations below the loose skin and then saw his fluid emerge in an arcing spray that landed on his shiny belly.

'That's better!' she cooed, wiping him with the flannel she'd kept in a bowl of warm water on the bedside table. She dusted him with talc, then dressed him in his silk pyjama trousers.

'Thank you, Nurse.'

Not knowing quite how to continue, Lynne tucked him into the bed and went into the bathroom to make herself ready for bed. While she brushed her teeth she could feel her body still ready for action, and hoped it wouldn't take Nick too long to get into the mood again. She washed carefully then rubbed her bosom with her own favourite body lotion. It felt so good that she lingered awhile, feeling her nipples grow firm once more in response to her oiled fingers, stroking the heavy undersides of her breasts where the sensation was delicate and subtle, making her vagina contract with sudden longing. Then, draping a black nylon negligée about her shoulders but leaving it open down the front, she returned to the bedroom.

Much to her dismay, Nick was already fast asleep and snoring.

Lynne retreated, unwilling to waken him or subject herself to sleep while she was still feeling so horny. Going into the spare room, she switched on the bedside lamp and lay down on the bed. There was an old-fashioned mirror on the dressing-table and she caught sight of herself in the black negligée, sprawled on the bed. Smiling at her own reflection, she swept her hand behind her head and thrust out her breasts in a sexy pose.

She looked good, as sexy as any model in a magazine. Slowly she began to finger herself, watching her labia grow redder, more moist, the lips swell and blossom under her careful caresses.

Lynne sighed with pleasure and saw her breasts heave, pushing their way out from beneath the scanty covering, the nipples huge and ripe.

The mirror was about the same shape as a television screen, and it was easy for Lynne to imagine herself in an episode of *Night Owls*. Although she knew they would never allow anything so overtly pornographic, she began to fantasise about a sex scene between Carol and one of the male actors. He would come into the room and find her masturbating, then take over himself. But who should it be? Somehow Blake wouldn't quite do. Not after his apparent rejection of her. Then the image of Jonathan swam into her mind and she felt her arousal quicken. Yes, he would do very well!

Lynne pictured him coming through the door, his blue eyes widening first in surprise and then delight at what he saw. Soon he would be on the bed, smiling as he removed her hand from between her legs and replaced it with his own. His mouth would come straight to her eager nipple, first licking it with the tip of his tongue then sucking on it more strongly, sending her into delicious paroxysms. Just thinking about it triggered the first shuddering foretaste of her climax. In the mirror she could see the thin film of sweat already forming between her breasts, and her labia were flushed a deep rose. Determined to keep her eyes open all the while, she let the pulsating waves of sharp sensation wash over her again and again until her hands dropped to her side and she flopped back exhausted.

Later, feeling slightly ashamed of herself, she crept back into bed beside a still sleeping Nick. She cuddled up to the warmth of his back, but felt a sadness overtake her. Were things really starting to fall apart? Their reconciliation seemed so fragile now.

When Lynne arrived at the studio next morning and found that Jonathan was absent that day she felt relieved. After using his image in her sexual fantasy she was nervous about seeing him again, unsure whether she could trust herself not to blush when she met him face to face.

Instead, she had an unexpected encounter with Blake. He came up to tell her what everyone else already knew. 'We're only filming for a couple of hours this morning. The technicians are in dispute, and we're all on half time. Our scene is scheduled, but not Carol's one with Megan.'

Lynne's face dropped. She'd worked hard to learn her lines. 'Really? What a shame.'

'Provided they get an agreement it's back to normal working tomorrow. How about a coffee now? I was just on my way.'

She followed him out to the canteen, where the others were already gathered, but after they'd bought their drinks he led her to an empty table. 'I've not had much of a chance to talk to you lately, Lynne. How's life?' he asked in his usual bluff tone. 'Always presuming you still have one, outside the walls of Studio B!'

Lynne grinned at him wryly. 'Sometimes I wish I could swap places with Carol. Her life seems so uncomplicated.'

'Ssh, don't let the scriptwriters hear you say that! Seriously though, Lynne, I can't help noticing that you seem a bit glum today. Everything okay at home?'

She shrugged. 'Not really.'

His expression grew more serious. 'Nothing I'm responsible for, I trust? Forgive me if I overstepped the mark, bringing you flowers that time. When you said you were getting a divorce I assumed your other half was out of the picture.'

'Yes, it wasn't your fault, really. We had split up when I first met you, but we decided to have a go at getting back together again. Only it's not working out very well.'

'These things seldom do.'

'Having my photo splashed all over "Soaplines" didn't help, of course.'

'Ah! Well, we've all been through that particular mill. Occupational hazard, you might say. But don't let it get you down. People have very short memories, fortunately.'

Lynne felt comforted by her brief conversation with Blake. He seemed to have reverted to the mentor rôle that he had adopted at the beginning, and she was glad that he was still prepared to be friends.

Carol had a scene with Hugo in the club. She had taken unofficial time off to go and see Andrew's girlfriend and her boss was none too pleased. Lynne found working with Blake easier after their chat at lunch and the scene went with considerable sparkle.

'Maybe I should put you over my knee and spank you,' Hugo threatened saucily.

Lynne did her best to look coy. 'If you do that I shall expect a rise,' Carol had to reply. 'I know that certain young ladies charge good money for that sort of thing.'

'Cheeky hussy! Just don't give me the excuse again, that's all!'

'Okay, cut!' yelled Don. 'Well done, you two.

There's quite a chemistry coming across – nice work!'

Lynne felt pleased with herself as she travelled home at midday. Although she didn't need others to tell her she had progressed with her acting it was always nice to receive praise from Don, who didn't hand it out lightly. What a pity Nick couldn't be more appreciative of her efforts, she thought sadly. Just lately he'd grown more grudging in his comments and sometimes it was hard to get him to even watch the programme. Last weekend he had sat there paying more attention to the crossword in his lap than the TV screen.

Maybe he was envious of her success. Lynne had always suspected that he couldn't take any competition from her, and that was why he'd stood in the way of her becoming more qualified. Yet she was convinced that her being on television had renewed Nick's interest. Turning into her street she gave a frustrated sigh. It seemed she couldn't put a foot right where her husband was concerned.

Lynne was surprised to see Nick's car parked outside their gate. He didn't usually come home for lunch. She let herself in and went through to the kitchen, but although two dirty glasses stood on the table he wasn't there. Frowning, she opened the door to the other rooms on the ground floor but there was no sign of him. She called up the stairs but, hearing no reply, went up to investigate.

The bathroom door was wide open so he wasn't in there either. As Lynne approached the bedroom, however, she began to hear sounds – shockingly familiar sounds. Something made her approach on tiptoe and pause outside the bedroom door. There were those noises again: harsh, rasping breath and the slight squeaking of bedsprings, then muffled speech. Lynne's heart was galloping in her chest as she took hold of the door knob and slowly turned it, opening the door a fraction and then a bit wider until she had a clear view of the bed.

Lying there in sensual abandon was a woman of about her own age. She had long dark hair and although her eyes were closed Lynne guessed that they were brown. Although she was still wearing a blouse it was completely open down the front and she wore no bra. Her shapely lips were parted in ecstasy and her bared breasts were full and erect, the tawny nipples provocatively exposed. Her skirt was up around her waist and, where her panties should be, Lynne saw her husband's head. He was lapping enthusiastically at the woman's pussy, making slurping noises and moaning with lust.

Lynne was filled with a poisonous disgust. She felt paralysed, unable to move or speak. Yet she was fascinated by the scene unfolding before her eyes.

Chapter Seven

IT DIDN'T TAKE Lynne very long to work out that the woman was Jenny. Although she'd never seen her husband's mistress, he had described her and it seemed unlikely that he would have had the time to get involved with anyone else. Angry as she was at this further betrayal, Lynne felt oddly comforted. Perhaps it was a case of 'better the she-devil you know . . .'

Except that it was hard to think of the woman lying in her bed as a devil. She had a sweetly pretty face, and the way she caressed Nick's curly head as he licked her suggested she was genuinely fond of him. Lynne wondered what to do. She couldn't bring herself to interrupt the proceedings, but neither could she tear herself away, so she was condemned to remain a voyeur. 'Condemned?' Lynne smiled to herself. Who was she trying to kid? No, she was actually enjoying the spectacle. There, she'd admitted it!

Jenny had to be almost at her climax. Her head was thrown right back, her thighs moved restlessly and she was flexing the toes of her right foot in a rhythmic way against Nick's buttocks. Lynne felt her own body becoming aroused as she imagined what the other woman must be feeling and when at last Jenny came, with a series of little cries, Lynne felt an answering throb in her groin and had to clutch at the door jamb for support.

Almost at once Nick hoisted himself up and plunged in with his rigid cock. Lynne recognised his groan of relief as he sank into the woman's body, and for a moment she felt a stab of jealousy. Why couldn't he have done that to her last night, when she really needed it? Had he been saving himself for this encounter with Jenny?

There were too many unanswered questions buzzing in Lynne's brain. She no longer felt able to stand and watch, but instead of bursting in on them she crept back downstairs and made herself a cup of tea. It was weird sitting there quietly, knowing full well what was going on in the room above, but for the moment that was all she wanted to do. Let them discover her presence in their own good time.

Soon there were unmistakable noises filtering down the stairs, the moans and gasps of a couple nearing their consummation. Lynne was still pondering how to react. She felt distant, unnaturally cool about the whole situation. It was almost as if she'd expected it to happen.

After a short silent interval she heard Jenny padding into the bathroom and calling, 'I'm going to be late!'

Nick reassured her. 'Don't worry, we'll get back on time. Like a quick coffee?'

'Yes, please!'

Lynne braced herself, awaiting the moment when her husband would enter the kitchen. She heard his heavy tread come down the stairs and then his gasp of horrified shock as he saw her sitting there, calmly drinking tea.

'Surprise, surprise!' She gave him a wry smile. 'Technicians are in dispute with Sphere, so they sent us home early.'

He still didn't know how much she knew. Lynne watched with amusement as he wondered frantically whether he could possibly get away with it. 'I . . . er . . . just popped home to pick up some papers. I think they must be upstairs. Won't be a tick.'

'It's all right, Nick, I know Jenny's up there. You've nothing to hide, I saw it all.'

'Oh God!'

He sank down on to a stool, covering his face with his hands. Lynne was amazed at how composed she was. 'Shall I make two coffees?' she offered.

Nick nodded, unable to look at her. While they were waiting for the kettle to boil, Jenny came down. Her face dropped when she saw the two of them. 'Oh dear!' she murmured, turning back towards the hall. 'Perhaps I'd better leave.'

Nick said nothing, so Lynne went over to the kettle and poured hot water onto the brown powder in two mugs. 'Wait a moment, Jenny,' she called. 'This is for you.'

Lynne was perversely enjoying the situation since she felt more in control than either of them. After all, she was in her own house and had done nothing wrong. She was almost gloating as the shame-faced pair sat uneasily on their stools, waiting for their drinks.

Lynne handed each of them a mug. 'Sugar?' she asked Jenny, who shook her head. 'No, I suppose you don't. Not with your figure.'

It was the first reference Lynne had made to anything physical, and she was rewarded by the sight of the other woman's red cheeks. Jenny gulped her drink down then rose awkwardly, evidently feeling she must say something conciliatory. 'I'm sorry, Lynne. Really I am.'

'Spare me the false apologies, at least!'

Lynne took their empty mugs to the sink and began to scrub them under the tap. She heard Nick mutter something and Jenny went out into the hall.

Nick came up to Lynne. He put a hand on her shoulder, but she shrugged it off. He said gruffly, 'We'll talk about this when I get back tonight, okay?'

'You intend to come back, then?'

He looked hurt. 'Obviously we need to talk. I'm sorry I've got to rush off right now, but we're both due back at work.'

The venom welled up in her. 'Well, I'm sorry you're reduced to lunch-hour quickies, Nick. Must be rather a come-down after living with the woman for two years.'

He began to say something then thought better of it and hurried from the kitchen. She heard the front door slam followed by his car revving outside, and an emptiness descended on the house that was mirrored in Lynne's soul. Slowly she made her way upstairs.

Her emotions were still confused, and her own behaviour puzzled her. How had she managed to remain so cool and collected? What was really disturbing was the thought that he could have been bringing Jenny back to the house on a regular basis, presumably because they both worked nearby. How long had it been going on? And why hadn't she ranted and raved at the pair of them? Maybe because she'd had a couple of years to get used to the idea of Nick screwing Jenny. In a weird way Lynne considered that the woman had almost as much right to him as she had. After all, her attempt at patching up her marriage hadn't been a great success.

Lynne reluctantly entered the bedroom. The sheet had been smoothed and the duvet rearranged, so she wouldn't have guessed that anything untoward had been going on. She took off all her clothes and lay down on the fitted sheet which was still warm and felt slightly damp halfway down the bed. The pillow smelt of Jenny's perfume, a flowery scent laced with spice that suggested a subtly feminine sexuality.

Lynne felt erotically charged when she thought of what she had viewed from the doorway, and she stretched her limbs languidly under the comforting duvet. Her hands found her breasts and began absently stroking her soft nipples, tweaking them into tight points. She could still see Jenny's large, shapely breasts thrusting towards the ceiling, their brownish tips peaking with desire, and she wondered how they would feel to her touch. Perhaps the feeling of being excluded from her husband's love play with his mistress had been the most painful one of all. With a shock she recognised that at some basic, but hitherto unacknowledged, level she had wanted to make it a threesome.

Reaching down between her thighs, Lynne found herself wet and open to her own fingers. She set about pleasuring herself in a fast and furious manner, feeling strangely empowered by her recent self-discovery. The friction she was applying to her already engorged clitoris made her wrist ache and her breath emerged in loud gasps, but she came in a few seconds with a series of rapid spasms that spent all her energy in one violent outpouring.

Utterly drained, Lynne fell asleep for a while. When she awoke it was four o'clock and she knew that Nick would be home in two hours. Going into the bathroom she took a shower and dressed in jeans and a sweater before going out to the supermarket. She bought steak and red wine, came home and set the table with candles and flowers. If they were going to 'talk things over' they might as well do it in style!

When her husband came home Lynne was wearing a slinky red jersey dress with lipstick to match. She was determined not to let the afternoon's episode damage her hard-won self-esteem. Nick appeared dazed as he sat down to the delicious meal she had prepared for him, but only when he'd taken a few sips of the wine did he pluck up the courage to ask, 'What's all this in aid of then, Lynne?'

'It's our anniversary. Had you forgotten?'

'Anniversary?' His face was screwed up with the effort of remembering. 'I thought we were married in June.'

'Yes, but you came back to me just one month ago today, in the Manor House Hotel. Remember now?'

He looked sheepish, muttering, 'Really, Lynne, do you think this is appropriate?'

'What would you prefer to happen?'

'Oh, I'm not complaining! Just mystified.'

'I know I'm not reacting as you might expect, but funnily enough I just don't feel particularly angry about what happened today. Maybe I half expected it.'

Nick put down his fork and took her hand. 'Look, love, I still want us to make a go of it, if we can. I know I've acted stupidly, but it won't happen again.'

'So you still want me, then?'

'Of course! Look, today was the first time I'd bedded Jenny since you and I got back together. It's the truth, I promise you. She wanted some advice on applying for promotion and I thought we could talk confidentially here.'

'But you were unable to resist her. I can understand that. She's a very pretty woman.'

'So are you, Lynne.'

She gave a resigned sigh. 'Okay, I'll forgive you this once. But there are conditions.'

'Oh?'

Throwing him a seductive look she promised, 'I'll tell you upstairs.'

Scenting some sport, Nick rose from the table and followed her. Lynne smiled to herself as she reviewed what she had in mind. When they were both in the bedroom she invited her husband to lie on the bed and watch while she undressed. Slowly she unzipped her dress and freed her arms from the sleeves so that the top fell down, exposing her naked breasts. 'Would you like to kiss them?' she asked coyly.

'You know I would!'

'All right. Then tell me about what you and Jenny like to do.'

Nick's face dropped. 'Hey! I thought I already told—'

'I said there were conditions, Nick, remember?'

'What is this?'

'Part of the deal. You tell me about the intimate

goings-on between you and her, then you have access to my body. But not before.'

He stared at her, weighing up the situation with a frown. 'But why, for God's sake?'

'I just want to know, that's all. This afternoon, when I watched you and Jenny making love, I felt excluded. I just want some of the mystery taken out of it. I don't want to feel jealous. I want to understand. For a while she was as big a part of your life as I'd been, and we can't simply shut her out and pretend she didn't happen. Don't you see, Nick, this is my way of trying to come to terms with it.'

Nick nodded, slowly. 'I can understand that. All right, then. Come here, and I'll tell you whatever you want to know.'

He reached up for her as she approached, his fingers caressing the side of her breast. Lynne felt a frisson of desire. She leaned forward and whispered, 'Tell me about one of the games you played with her.'

Nick had both of her breasts in his palms now, weighing them. He kissed each of the elongated nipples in turn, then began to talk in a low voice.

'One of her favourites we used to call "on the beach". She'd get into her bikini and lie on the bed with the sunlamp on, wearing sunglasses. I'd be in the shower wearing swim-trunks and getting wet all over. Then I'd come out as if I'd just been in the sea, and she'd ask me to rub suntan oil over her, starting with her back. She liked me to push down her bikini pants and oil her. I'd sneak a finger into her from time to time. She loved that.'

'And did you go on holiday together, to a real beach, I mean?'

'Only once. It was great, but she wanted to re-live

it over and over. I got tired of that game after a while.'

Lynne could feel herself yearning for greater stimulation herself. She pulled her dress down and wriggled out of it, then lay down wearing only her bikini-style pants. 'Pretend I'm on the beach now,' she told him. 'You can oil my breasts. There's some stuff in the bathroom.'

Nick seemed happy enough to comply. He found her favourite body mousse. It felt light and tickly on her nipples when he first squirted it on her, but soon dissolved into a delightfully smooth and exotically scented oil. With her eyes closed, Lynne could almost imagine herself on that sun-drenched beach. She knew just how Jenny must have felt.

'All right,' she murmured, when other parts of her body were clamouring for attention. 'Now you can tell me about something else. Her underwear. Did she like to wear any while you made love?'

'Oh yes. She had a black leather bikini that she put on sometimes. There was a studded leather collar, too.'

'That sounds exciting. Did she dominate you?'

'Kind of. She always wanted to be on top when she was wearing that outfit, anyway.'

'What – like this?'

Deftly Lynne slid from underneath him and pinned his legs between her thighs. He laughed. 'Not quite! I wouldn't have all these clothes on, for a start.'

'That can soon be remedied.'

She stripped off his shirt and trousers, but left his pants on for the time being. The bulge in them made her feel hornier than ever, but she knew she must exercise restraint if she wanted to find out more about him and Jenny. 'So, what did she do?'

'It was more what she made me do. Like rubbing her here, for example.'

He reached down and found Lynne's swelling clitoris through the cotton of her panties, then proceeded to rub until her juices soaked through.

'What else did she wear?' Lynne asked, faintly.

'She had this pink velvet body. We both liked that because it opened at the crotch with three poppers, and I could get in easily. It was also a bit small for her, so her boobs were squashed into the top and gave her a good cleavage. She could bring me off with that cleavage.'

Lynne realised that, despite his earlier reluctance, Nick was enjoying telling her all this. She gave a triumphant smile. Her instinct had been right. If she could get Nick to divulge all the secrets of his sex-life with Jenny then she could end up satisfying him completely, making sure that the other woman had no more power over him. The thought was exciting her further. She quickly removed her panties and slid onto his more than adequate erection, sighing as the exquisite sensations flooded through her, making her vagina clamp eagerly on to his tumid penis and hold him for a while, flexing her muscles to stimulate her own erect clitoris. She leaned forward and he took one of her breasts in his mouth, licking her nipple greedily.

'Now tell me, Nick, how did you like it when she was inside you – fast or slow?'

'Both. Usually starting off slow then speeding up.'

Lynne willingly complied, at first barely moving but all the while savouring the subtle increase in her own arousal. She could have forced the pace to satisfy her own urges, but she wanted to hold back.

Nick had told her that Jenny usually took a long time to come, and sometimes didn't make it. She wanted to know how that felt.

'Did you talk to her while you were fucking?' she asked him.

'Yes.'

'What about?'

'Sometimes about you.'

Lynne was so startled she nearly let him slip out of her. It simply hadn't occurred to her that Jenny might have been equally curious about her. She squeezed onto him, feeling the electric thrill as the nerves of her clitoris buzzed hotly. Then she said, 'Okay, pretend I'm Jenny. What would you say about me?'

A smile spread across Nick's face and he pulled at her breasts to make her lean forward. He took each of her nipples into his mouth in turn, sucking them like fruit. 'Ask me nicely.'

'Please, Nick, won't you tell me what your wife was like in bed?'

'I'll tell you if you promise to squash my dick between your gorgeous breasts afterwards and bring me off.'

A shudder went through Lynne from top to bottom. She murmured her assent, and Nick continued his soft handling of her breasts accompanied by the occasional upward thrust of his penis. 'Well, she was very easy to arouse, for one thing.'

'Easier than me?'

'Yes. She came more quickly, sometimes more than once. And she liked it up, down and sideways. But we never played the kind of games you and I play. It was always straight sex, nothing more.'

'But you like what we do together, don't you Nick?'

'Oh, yes! They say the mind is the ultimate erogenous zone, don't they?'

'Do you ever think of her while you're making love to me, then?'

'Sometimes.'

'You imagine I'm her?'

'That would be difficult.'

'Why?'

'Well, you've got bigger breasts, for a start. And you talk to me more. She used to go off into a world of her own.'

'Did she have fantasies?'

'I don't know, I never asked.'

Lynne giggled. 'Well, I bet she did! I bet she imagined you were Tom Cruise, or someone.'

'You could be right. It doesn't bother me. Half the time I was with her I was dreaming of you – after we'd met, of course.'

Lynne felt her bubble burst a little. She didn't like to think of those fraught days when she suspected that Nick was having an affair but hadn't known for sure.

Still, they were playing a game of verbal tit for tat and it was her turn. Smiling sweetly she said, 'Are you quite sure your wife has never faked an orgasm?'

Nick was visibly ruffled. 'As far as I know she didn't need to.'

'But how would you know?'

'All I know is, she never complained.'

'Ah!'

He was starting to play rough with her breasts, kneading them and pinching her nipples quite hard.

Lynne felt the swirling currents begin that usually drove her towards her climax but she held herself back, wanting a slower pace. She was exploring Jenny's psyche through Nick, and that meant changing sexually. Quite how she wasn't sure, but the process was certainly exciting. She stilled her movements and let the throbbing tide wash through her, warm and sweet, while Nick's hands swept slowly over her breasts and stomach then reached behind to clutch her buttocks.

'Tell me,' she began again. 'Did she feel the same as me – inside, I mean?'

'Not quite. I suppose she was always readier for me than you are. By the time I got into her she was always very wet, whereas you're often quite tight.'

Lynne contracted her vagina over his prick. 'Like this, you mean?'

'Mm!'

'And did she like to give head?'

'Yes.'

'Did she swallow?'

'Sometimes.'

'Which would you rather have, honestly now, a blow job or a boob job?'

'Do I have to choose?'

'I just wondered which you liked best.'

'They're both good. Talking of which, didn't you promise me something if I told you about her?'

Lynne eased herself off his erection and knelt over his thighs, pushing her breasts together. Nick took his cock and placed it in her cleavage. She proceeded to massage it with her breasts, but she felt awkward and not particularly aroused herself. Then he suggested that she should lie down and let him to the work, which was a lot easier.

Soon he was thrusting up towards her face between the twin globes. Looking down she could see the pearly drop in the slit, and knew that it wouldn't be long before he came. She pressed her chin down and put out her tongue to see if she could lick him. The top of his penis was sticky with juice. Lynne thumbed her nipples as she held her breasts firmly, beginning to enjoy the friction which was setting up reverberations below. His balls were slapping hard against her stomach as he approached his climax at speed, and when he started to come she let the whole of his glans enter her mouth so that she could taste the salty stream as it shot down her throat. There, she thought aggressively, that's something you were never prepared to do for him, Miss Megaboobs!

Afterwards, when Nick had recovered, Lynne asked him to return the favour.

'Sometimes I think this is what Jenny liked best,' he told her, as he slid down her body, paying glancing obeisance to her breasts before nuzzling in her mound. 'She loved it when I went down on her for hours on end.'

Lynne lay back voluptuously, relishing the cool touch of his tongue as it snaked its way in through her labia to drink from her sex. Normally she would have thrust herself against him, craving more intense feeling, wanting to hasten her climax. This time, though, she remained relaxed. She needed to know how it felt to be totally passive, to let it all flow without any input from squeezing thighs or thrusting pelvis. She wanted to be the way she imagined Jenny was, hard to arouse but sensual and feminine, a challenge to a man and therefore, ultimately, more of a reward.

For a while it was hard just to lie there, telling herself she didn't have to do anything, letting Nick indulge her because she didn't have to prove anything to him any more. Remembering how desperately she had tried to please him during the last, failing months of their marriage Lynne felt sad and obscurely ashamed. Now she could legitimately queen it over him because, once again, he'd chosen her rather than his mistress.

The feelings that Nick's gentle lips and tongue were inducing in her were delicate and kept her hovering on the edge of frustration, but she was learning to renounce the crude urgency of her longing in favour of a finer appreciation of the pleasures of the flesh. She knew that her clitoris was swollen and exposed but without direct stimulation it merely kept a tingling heat circling around her vulva. Sighing with delight she stroked his head, the way she had seen Jenny do, and he reached up to fondle her breasts.

Soon Lynne was completely mellowed out, floating on a sensual sea that uplifted her without pushing her in any particular direction. Nick was slipping a fingertip inside her from time to time, and a pool of liquid was gathering at her entrance which he was licking up but always there was more ready to flow. Her tender parts were completely enveloped in the sweet juices and felt like warm velvet, inside and out. Then she felt his tongue make direct contact with her clitoris.

Lynne cried out as the keen spasm shook her, but he moved away and she relaxed again into the state of dreamy eroticism she'd been in before. Yet now she could feel the hunger just below the surface, the need to increase the pace that would not be denied. She forced herself to lie still, leaving it to Nick to find his way back to the centre of her pleasure in his own good time.

He didn't keep her waiting long. Next time he plugged her with his finger, she felt his tongue part her labia and deliberately seek out her waiting clitoris. It rose to meet him, expanding and pulsating with unashamed passion, starting her off on a dizzying spiral of intense feeling that left her breathless. Sensing that she needed more stimulation now, Nick licked her rapidly while he plunged his finger in and out of her vagina, and Lynne knew that it was no use trying to hold back any longer.

The first shivers of her orgasm took her by surprise, escalating quickly into a strong and satisfying pulse that pounded throughout her body in hot waves. Lynne delivered herself up to the ecstasy, letting it free her, take her wherever it wanted. The climax went on longer than usual, holding her in suspension for a long series of delicious, seemingly endless moments, then letting her down gently, decreasing almost imperceptibly. From somewhere inside her head Lynne thought she heard herself say, 'Oh Nick, that was wonderful!' and she heard him grunt contentedly in reply.

The sleep that followed was deeply fulfilling. Lynne woke in the night, remembered what had happened, and promptly fell back to sleep again with a smile on her lips. She awoke to find Nick nuzzling at her breast but, glancing at the alarm clock, realised she had forgotten to set it, and would be late.

'God! I've got ten minutes to be out of the house!' she exclaimed, rushing to the bathroom.

There was no time to reflect on what had happened between her and Nick once she arrived at the studio.

Jonathan greeted her with the news that the technicians had resolved their dispute, but two days' filming had to be squashed into one to keep the soap on schedule. With studio time at a premium there was no room for mistakes and everyone had to concentrate really hard on their lines. Lynne heaved a sigh of relief when she got through her two scenes without having to do any re-takes.

Once the hectic day was over, however, Lynne couldn't wait to get back home. There was still a slight uneasiness within her, a mild foreboding that wouldn't go away until she had been reassured that everything really was all right again. The rôle-play that she and Nick had indulged in had helped dispel any lingering feelings of jealousy towards Jenny. Even so, she didn't feel totally secure. The pair of them could have discussed the situation over coffee, or during lunch, and come to some new agreement that excluded her. Perhaps she would always feel vulnerable as long as her husband worked in the same firm as his mistress.

The house seemed quiet when she opened the front door, even though she was almost an hour later than usual. There was no sign of Nick's car. Her doubts returned, redoubled. She walked into the kitchen and then stopped in her tracks, letting out a gasp of outrage. There, sitting in poised silence on a stool, was Jenny.

'What the hell are you doing here?' Lynne snapped, reverting to a primal, territorial anger.

'Look, Lynne, I'm sorry about this. I know it's a shock but I wanted to talk to you.'

'Where's Nick?'

'At the pub. It was his idea that I should see you. Alone.'

Jenny looked very different with clothes on. She wore a trim powder blue suit with nothing visible beneath. The vee neck showed off her deep cleavage, and Lynne found it hard to take her eyes off the voluptuous swell of her bosom. She could feel her cheeks heating up as last night's proceedings played back in her head.

'Maybe you could do with a drink?' Jenny suggested. 'I brought some wine.'

She held up a bottle of Australian chardonnay with a tentative smile. Lynne retorted, spitefully, 'I'd rather have a cup of tea.'

While she went over to put the kettle on, still seething, Lynne was filled with an electric excitement. She was already planning what she would do if Jenny tried to pull rank on her. She wouldn't give up without a fight – literally. It wouldn't take much to topple the woman to the floor. Lynne briefly relished the thought of mussing up that prissy French plait, smearing that red lipstick all over her cheeks, making her mascara run with tears of pain.

'Would you mind if I had a glass of wine? I don't drink tea.'

Lynne gave a shrug. She began to tell her where the glasses were but Jenny was already halfway to the cupboard. 'Oh, of course you know your way around. I'd forgotten.'

Jenny gave her a sympathetic look. 'I'm sorry, Lynne. I know this isn't easy for you, but you're in a stronger position than me right now, believe me.' She poured herself a glass of the wine and gulped it down. 'Dutch courage!' she said, with a grin.

Despite herself, Lynne began to warm to her. In other circumstances they might have been friends.

She made herself a mug of tea then went to stand against the door, guardedly, taking a small sip of the hot liquid. She grimaced: she had made it in haste, and it was too weak.

Jenny was looking at her frankly, her brown eyes soft and velvety but with something more complex hidden in their depths. 'Look, I won't beat about the bush. Nick said you were curious about me. It's understandable. I feel the same about you. We both love Nick . . .'

'If you're going to suggest some kind of fifty-fifty arrangement, you can save your breath!' Lynne snapped.

'Not exactly. Not in the way you probably mean, at any rate. It was Nick's idea, but he thought it would be better coming from me. Do you know what a *ménage à trois* entails?'

Lynne stared at her, unbelieving. 'He suggested that?'

'Only if you're willing. He is, and so am I, but it has to be agreed by all three of us, obviously, and I suppose there would have to be some rules. You don't have to decide straight away, but I'd be grateful if you could think it over. It could be the ideal solution.'

Chapter Eight

'I THINK I will have that glass of wine now.'

Lynne poured a generous measure from the bottle that Jenny handed her, then suggested they should go through to the sitting room. Her mind was still reeling from the proposal, and she needed time to think. Watching the other woman settle herself in an armchair near the window, Lynne found herself speculating about what she would be like to make love with. She'd never thought about another woman as a sex object before, but somehow it seemed perfectly natural to be regarding Jenny in that way. She had a full and sensual mouth, lovely hair that would be nice to touch when it was flowing free, and a sexy figure. Nick knew that body inside out, as he knew hers. And both women knew his, equally intimately. So why shouldn't that love triangle be completed?

'I don't quite know how to proceed,' Jenny admitted, sipping nervously at her glass. 'I mean, you hardly know me. Except what you've heard about me from Nick.'

Lynne thought she saw a sly little smile crinkling

the corners of those glossy lips. Surely Nick hadn't told her about last night? She felt a tell-tale flush creep up her cheeks and cursed inwardly. Was that why he'd made his suggestion, because he thought she wanted to take her curiosity about Jenny to its logical conclusion?

Lynne watched her gulp down more wine. They were eyeing each other like wary beasts. Then Jenny said, 'You haven't thrown me out yet, anyway! I take that as a good sign.'

'Nick told you to wait here for him, did he?'

She nodded. 'Unless you show me the door, in which case I'm to meet him at the Dog and Whistle.'

'I see. You two have it all planned out, don't you?'

'Not really.' Jenny uncrossed her shapely legs, making a rustle of silk on silk. 'The idea of us all living together is almost as new to me as it is to you, and I must say I have my own misgivings about it.'

'You do?'

'Of course!' Her tone was sharp, letting Lynne know she was not to be taken lightly. 'If I'm to give up my independence I'd want to be sure it would work out, at least for a while.'

'How could one be sure?'

'We both love Nick, don't we? That's a good start. And I've never borne you any ill will, Lynne. So I'm prepared to give it a go if you are. We wouldn't rush into it. Maybe I could just stay the night a couple of times, until we all got used to the idea.'

'What's the alternative?'

Jenny sighed, turning to gaze through the window at the evening light. 'I suppose it would mean Nick having to choose between us. But whoever he chose would have no guarantees. I suppose I see this as a chance for us all to have what we want.'

'Don't you think it sounds a bit too good to be true?'

'Maybe. But you don't have to decide now. Take your time. Meanwhile, can't we just be friends? I'm dying to know what it's like to be in *Night Owls*!'

Her open enthusiasm was endearing. As Lynne chatted with more confidence, she found herself thinking about the situation from the other woman's angle. Maybe Jenny had envied Lynne her marriage, the day-to-day security and relaxed intimacy – until things had started to go wrong, of course.

She also began to understand what Nick had seen in Jenny. She had an attractive voice, honeyed and mellow, and she emitted a genuine warmth that cut through barriers. Lynne could feel her interest in the woman growing, and with it a faint stirring of her desire. It was even possible to envisage being in bed with her, cuddling and giggling, in sisterly communion.

The front room quickly became a gossip parlour, and after an hour or so of heart-to-heart conversation Lynne didn't find it in the least untoward when Jenny asked to see her wedding photos. When Nick walked in some time later he found them both on the floor with the album open, shrieking with laughter.

Jenny was the first to see him. 'Nick, you never told me you used to have just a moustache! You look like Ed Cartwright!'

'Oh no!' he groaned.

Lynne was puzzled. 'Who's he?'

'Oh, someone at work,' Jenny said.

Despite herself, Lynne felt slightly piqued. Was this what it would be like if Jenny moved in, constant little reminders of the fact that they shared a life apart from her? But then Nick squatted down and put his arms around them both, kissing each on the cheek in turn. 'My two lovely ladies,' he murmured. 'God, I'm such a lucky man!'

At first, Lynne felt a frisson of tension as the three of them were physically close for the first time. She put an arm around Jenny to complete the circle, and felt them all relax. Nick hugged them, then got up. 'Any wine left, girls, or have you drunk me out of house and home?'

He opened another bottle and, as she downed her third glass, it occurred to Lynne that sex might be on the cards that very night. Jenny was making no moves to leave, and Nick looked extremely happy to be there with both of them. She knew that the decision must come from her, and her instinct was to go along with the experiment. One more glass of wine and she might even initiate it.

Lynne caught Nick glancing lustfully at Jenny's cleavage. He looked at his wife and winked. There was a glint of amusement in his eyes that drew her in and gave her confidence, so that she no longer felt threatened. She even began to fantasise about their joint seduction of Jenny. After all, she was supposed to be hard to arouse . . .

Jenny went up to the bathroom, leaving them alone. Nick raised his brows at Lynne as he took her hand. 'Well?'

She giggled. 'I think I quite fancy her!'

He smiled, drawing her into his arms. 'Is that a "yes" then?'

'Mm. I think so.'

He kissed her on the forehead. 'Thank God! I don't know what I'd have done if you'd refused.

I've been dreaming about it ever since last night.'

'Shall we ask her to stay tonight?'

'If you like. I certainly feel like it!'

They were kissing passionately when Jenny returned. Lynne heard her say, ironically, 'Do I leave now – or join in?'

Nick held out his hand to her, smiling. 'I think you can stay. Okay, Lynne?'

She knew she had to do something to indicate her willingness. Taking Jenny in her arms Lynne slowly lowered her lips on to hers. It felt strange, deep kissing another woman. Jenny's mouth was soft and yielding under her own. She could feel Nick's hands on her breasts, seeking her nipples beneath the T-shirt she was wearing, making her long for more contact. Her own hands were on Jenny's slim waist, and she was wondering if she dared move down to caress her buttocks in the tight-fitting suit. What she really wanted was to undo the buttons of her jacket, but she felt it would be too forward. Just what was the etiquette when making love in a threesome? She decided to let the other two make the running as far as possible.

The interplay of their tongues was becoming bolder, giving Lynne the encouragement she needed to move her hands down on to Jenny's tight little bum. Through the linen fabric she could feel the smooth tautness of her buttocks with the cleft between. The other woman mirrored her movements, clutching at her own behind while they kissed yet more passionately, and Lynne knew she had nothing to fear. All was permissible. Her hands moved further down, just below the protruberance of Jenny's behind, and she felt the knobbly presence of suspenders. It was a pleasantly familiar feeling, since she enjoyed wearing stockings herself.

They drew breath and Nick took the opportunity to pull Lynne's top off, exposing her pink lace bra. It was the cue she needed. Looking into Jenny's dark eyes, she undid the fabric-covered top button of her suit. The plump lips widened into a smile, and Lynne quickly undid the other three, then Nick took her jacket off and laid it over the back of a chair.

Jenny's breasts looked magnificent in a black basque. They were pushed up to accentuate her cleavage, and through the lace Lynne could just see the top of each pink areola. Something tweaked her inside, a sharp spasm that made her gasp and fuelled her growing desire to explore the other woman's body more thoroughly. She watched as Jenny undid her hair from the French plait and let it come tumbling down in glorious abandon around her shoulders.

Nick's desire was obvious too. He had undone his fly and was pressing his bursting erection against Lynne's thigh so that she could feel its insistent hardness even through her jeans. He undid her belt and button then slid down her zip, so that she could step out of them. Then he helped Jenny to get out of her skirt.

In the figure-cinching basque her body looked trim and wonderfully erotic. The combination of long hair and corsetry gave her an old-fashioned look, like a Victorian pin-up. She was a couple of inches shorter than Lynne, and with such a small frame that her breasts seemed outsize. Enviously Lynne watched her husband lick his way down Jenny's cleavage and felt momentarily excluded – but not for long. Kneeling down, she eased the stocking tops out of their suspenders and rolled them down, kissing each expanse of smooth thigh as she did so. Between the dangling suspenders she could see a pair of black silk panties.

Still at ground level, Lynne took the opportunity to free Nick from his trousers. The temptation to reach inside his bulging pants and feel his hot penis proved too great and he groaned with lust as she fetched out his prick and gave it a preliminary lick. It strained upwards, longing to be somewhere warm and wet. Inside her own pants Lynne could feel her equally erect clitoris spring into throbbing life, with the thin cotton of her panties clinging to the moistening folds. If she didn't get some direct stimulation there soon she would die of frustration!

It was Jenny who made the next move. When Nick went behind her to unzip her basque she reached round and unhooked Lynne's bra.

'Oh, what pretty breasts!' she exclaimed, feeling them delicately. She traced a path around their fullness then squeezed them gently. Lynne almost fainted with the sudden upsurge of her libido. When Nick succeeded in freeing Jenny from her corset and her beautiful bosom was fully exposed, Lynne returned the compliment.

'They're so firm,' she said wonderingly, her hands cupping the heavy undersides of Jenny's breasts. The taut flesh was springy under her fingers, and the nipples already half-swollen into the size and shape of soft berries. Unable to resist the urge, Lynne bent her head and took one of them in her mouth. Jenny gave a low moan and her nipple hardened instantly, growing huge and rigid as her nerve-endings responded to the sudden stimulus. Lynne felt her own breasts being fondled more urgently, and another hand had got into her panties from the back and was stroking the soft skin of her buttocks and fingering her anus.

For the first time she didn't know whose hands or lips were where and, more to the point, she didn't care. Somehow all three of them managed to sink to the floor simultaneously, and then it became a real free-for-all. Lynne found herself nuzzling at Jenny's hot crotch while Nick pulled her panties right down and was bathing her clitoris with her own love-juice. Then she became aware that there was no longer any barrier between her mouth and the soft fuzz of Jenny's pubis. For the first time in her life she found herself mouthing another woman's pussy.

The musky smell was overwhelming, but Lynne felt reassured by the fact that it was her own smell too. Tentatively she ran the tip of her tongue along the groove between the two labia, finding the nub at the top already standing proud of the inner lips. She reached up across the smooth expanse of stomach to the undersides of Jenny's breasts and stroked them softly while she made equally gentle lickings with her tongue. At the same time she was aware of Nick's mouth at her own sex, opening her up to his questing tongue.

At first it felt really strange to have her tongue poking into another woman's sex while Nick entered hers in similar fashion, but once she got used to the idea she really liked it. Whatever her husband did to her, she would do to Jenny. Before long she could feel both of their pleasure-buds swelling and throbbing in unified response to the rhythmic licking, and when Nick's finger came right inside her she did the same to Jenny and felt a twitch of response. As she sensed the woman becoming more and more aroused her own feelings intensified, so that she was soon on the verge of a climax.

The orgasm took her by surprise as she had been focusing more on what she was doing to Jenny. Gasping out her ecstasy, she tore her mouth away from the juicy folds and found herself biting into the soft flesh of Jenny's thigh, unable to help herself. There was a sharp groan from above, and then Lynne collapsed between the outspread thighs as the last racking spasms hit her. She was aware of Nick stroking her buttocks as the last sweet tremors faded, and then warm arms encircled her in their embrace.

'Let's help Jenny now, shall we?' she heard him whisper in her ear.

Dimly Lynne was aware of her husband mounting his mistress and pushing his erection hard into her. She opened her eyes and saw Jenny's smile, her hips jerking in time to his thrusting. Easing herself up alongside the woman's body, she placed her hands on both breasts, enjoying the solid feel of their shapely contours. She squeezed them hard and Jenny moaned softly, evidently liking it, so she did it again and then took one of the nipples between her lips. Greedily she sucked at it, watching Jenny squirm with delight, while her long hair brushed in silky swathes against her thighs.

Already Lynne could feel herself swelling urgently again between her wet labia. Reaching down she found it was possible to rub herself and Jenny at the same time, while her mouth remained at the enticing breast. One of her fingers wormed its way through the other woman's matted pubic hair to find the slickened clitoris, just out of reach of Nick's penis, and she proceeded to give it extra stimulation to propel Jenny towards her climax while she kept her own on hold. The increasing moans of satisfaction that filtered down to her were proof that the twin approach of Nick's lusty tool and her own willing hands and lips would soon achieve the desired result.

This time it was easy for Lynne to pace herself so that she remained in tune with both her partners. She had only to rub a little harder on Jenny's clitoris to bring her along, and a little softer on her own if she found herself jumping ahead. Knowing from experience that Nick would come when the pussy he was penetrating began to convulse around his penis, Lynne took her cue from the rising tide of Jenny's arousal. When her breasts were straining tightly and her clitoris was throbbing and huge, she suddenly sensed that the woman's whole body had tensed in the few seconds prior to her climax. Rubbing herself more rapidly, Lynne soon had herself in the same state and as the first gasps issued from Jenny's lips she felt her second climax start.

Three bodies seemed to vibrate as one while the orgasmic energy flowed through them, and Lynne felt the same warm benevolence envelop them all. The voluptuous harmony this produced was incredibly fulfilling. She found herself stroking Jenny's and Nick's bodies indiscriminately, caressing thighs, buttocks and breasts, prolonging the sense of oneness until she could feel nothing but a residual glow of utter contentment. Then they all tumbled together in a spent heap.

Nick was the first to speak. 'Wow!' he sighed. 'That exceeded all my expectations. You are two fantastic women!'

Jenny giggled. 'Don't pretend you didn't know it

all along!' Then she looked straight at Lynne. 'Thank you,' she said quietly.

Lynne saw an intimate acceptance of her, and heard an undertone of admiration in the other woman's voice that was extremely satisfying. She leaned over and kissed her tenderly on the cheek, her hands plunging into the dark silk curtain of her hair.

'Well, I don't know about you two but I'm starving!' Nick declared as he got to his feet. 'What do you say to an express pizza for three? Or we could go out for a meal, if you'd prefer.'

Both women voted to phone for a take-away. Lynne sensed that Jenny, like herself, was unwilling to risk breaking the atmosphere that their love-making had induced. As she munched on her share of the giant pizza she felt happier than she'd done for years. It really seemed as if this *ménage à trois* idea might work.

After their meal Nick suggested a communal shower. The three of them could scarcely fit into the cubicle at the same time, so they took it in turns. First Lynne and Nick soaped each other with luxurious gel while Jenny watched from the warm, scented waters of the bath. It didn't take long for Nick to get a huge erection, and while he caressed the stiff points of Lynne's slippery, aroused breasts she used her fingers deftly on his penis until he came in a series of sharp gasps, his semen spurting from him and mingling with the torrent of water from above.

'Your turn, Jen,' he smiled, once he'd recovered. 'I need a good soak.'

She got out of the bath slowly, her large breasts still glistening with foam, and Lynne felt a thrill of anticipation when she saw the look on the other woman's face, sultry and seductive. Jenny entered the shower smiling, then gave her a long, slow kiss on the mouth. She'd cleaned her teeth after the pizza and tasted of peppermint. The water rained down on them gently, beating a faint tattoo on their breasts. Lynne was tingling all over, partly with the invigorating effect of the shower but mostly with sexual desire. Any lingering inhibitions about lesbian love were quickly dispelled as Jenny's hands roved freely over her wet body, rubbing in the scented gel. Soon they were embracing and kissing with unfettered passion, and then Lynne felt a slippery finger enter her and the thumb of the same hand found her pulsating clitoris and began to work it while the finger plunged in and out.

Lynne was astonished at the speed with which she responded to Jenny's manual dexterity. Her curiosity about the woman grew. Surely she'd done this before? The woman's expertise was bringing her close to a climax already, and when Lynne felt warm lips against her breast and then enclosing her ripe nipple she cried out with the sudden intensification of her pleasure. The droplets rained down on her upturned face as, with shuddering breasts and thighs, she gave herself up to the sweet paroxysms that pulsed through her entire body.

She sank back, exhausted, and after a while felt Jenny drying her feet with a fluffy towel and massaging them with oil. Opening her eyes, Lynne saw that Nick was out of the bath and was kneeling behind his mistress, oiling her generous breasts from behind with his flattened palms. He smiled at her over Jenny's shoulder.

'I knew you two would get on well. You're both

demons when you get going.'

Lynne caught Jenny's eye. She was looking up at her almost coyly and Lynne felt a strange feeling hit her, as if the two women were in love and Nick was the outsider. It only lasted a second, but it was unsettling. She put it down to the situation being new and strange to her.

The interplay between the three of them moved on, and before long Nick was lying on his back being ministered to by his two women. Jenny knelt behind his head and stroked warm oil into his chest and shoulders, while Lynne massaged his thighs and kept an eye on his growing erection. When his penis was fully extended she took it between her oiled palms and rubbed it gently, moving down to caress his balls from time to time. Jenny eyed her enviously but made no move to usurp her position.

At last Nick said, 'Why don't you get on top of me, Lynne, while I give Jenny what she wants. I can tell you're both dying for it, and so am I!'

Jenny was light enough to perch on his chest with her knees over his shoulders. With a couple of folded towels behind his head, this gave Nick access to her open pussy, which he proceeded to lick enthusiastically. Lynne lowered herself carefully on to his robust member and sighed with relief as his full-blown erection filled her aching vagina. It seemed quite natural that while she rose and fell in a slow rhythm she should embrace Jenny from the rear and clasp her breasts, fingering the large nipples until she moaned aloud, leaning her head back until it was resting on Lynne's left shoulder.

At the zenith of her movements, Lynne found she could catch sight of them in the mirror of the bathroom cabinet. It was an extraordinary vision, and far more erotic than any she had seen in magazines or in naughty videos. The voluptuous image of the two women riding the rampant male would have made a fantastic photo. She could see Jenny's pink, squashed nipples peeping through her fingers as she tweaked them mercilessly. Her mouth was open, her eyes closed and her overall expression one of extreme sensual enjoyment. Lynne could plainly see Nick's tongue applying rapid friction to Jenny's sex and although his magnificent organ was necessarily invisible, its presence was strongly indicated by the look of rapture on Lynne's own face.

After just a few glimpses of the tantalisingly suggestive scene Lynne could hold out no longer and came in a great powerful surge that had her squeezing Nick's shaft over and over, triggering him into climaxing with her. She reached down and found Jenny's rigid clitoris between the soft petals of her labia, then began rolling it between the thumb and forefinger of one hand while she pinched Jenny's long, taut nipple with the other. Soon she felt shudders run through the other woman's body too. Once again they had peaked more or less in harmony, and when Jenny flopped, exhausted, against her Lynne felt a surge of satisfaction.

The three of them ended up in bed together, cuddling up beneath the duvet. It reminded Lynne of holidays spent as a child with her two cousins in their country home. A great cosy warmth enveloped her, something more than physical. It was the kind of feeling she got as a kid from her thumb and her security blanket. Sandwiched between Nick and Jenny was like being with her parents in their big bed, and it soon brought sweet dreams.

*

On the way to the studio next morning Lynne felt as if she had taken on another new identity. She was used to being 'Carol' by now, but this was different. She felt as if all her old emotions and habits had been rearranged overnight, turning her into a totally new person. For one thing she'd discovered that she could share Nick, truly share him, and not feel jealous or insecure. It was a kind of maturity, giving her an inner strength.

Lynne had thought she was keeping her new life secret, but almost as soon as she arrived at the Sphere building Jonathan gave her a quizzical look.

'You look very pleased with yourself this morning, Lynne. Had some good news?'

She smiled back, glad that he'd picked up on her mood although she had no intention of revealing what had caused it. 'Not exactly. But you're right, I am in a good mood. Let's hope nothing happens to spoil it.'

'Watch out for Don, then. He's on the rampage. Blake's got into "Soaplines" again, this time over some dubious club he's supposed to frequent. Oh well, I suppose it'll all blow over.'

Lynne found it hard to concentrate on her lines and fluffed them several times. By the end of the afternoon she felt cross with herself and really fed up. Her heart hadn't been in her acting. She hoped it was only a temporary state of affairs.

'What you need is a boost from the scriptwriters,' Jonathan told her, after they'd called into the pub for a quick drink when the long day was over. 'I can tell you're getting fed up with serving behind the bar. Maybe they'll write you in a lover, or something.'

'Any chance of influencing them in that direction, do you think?'

Jonathan pulled a wry face. 'I should tread carefully if I were you. Chances are if you ask for a bit of action they'll put you through some gruesome accident. They're like that, contrary creatures. I remember when Sara complained that Megan was a boring character they made her illegitimate daughter crawl out of the woodwork then promptly had her killed off in a fire!'

'Any idea what their plans for Andrew are?'

Jonathan shook his head. 'I don't ask. As long as he stays in the soap I don't care what happens to him. He can spend the rest of his days head to foot in plaster and sitting in a wheelchair for all I care.'

'Like Sandy in *Crossroads*? You don't mean that! I mean, what chance would you get to show off your brilliant acting then?'

'Oh, I don't know. I could upstage Roger Moore's eyebrows, I suppose.'

Lynne laughed. Being with Jonathan always cheered her up. Without him her adjustment to the artificial world of television, and to the even weirder world of *Night Owls*, would have been much more difficult. They hardly ever talked personally, yet if she were ever in trouble he was one of the few people she would turn to and that made him a real friend.

On her way home Lynne began to feel excited at the thought of what she might be returning to. Had Nick and Jenny been planning some kind of surprise? She wouldn't put it past them to arrange some sexy game for them all to play. She had quite a few ideas of her own, mostly involving the two women ganging up on Nick in some way. Lynne smiled to herself as she turned into her road. Maybe her husband would get more than he'd bargained for in setting up their unconventional household!

Although Nick's car was parked outside, the house was quiet. So quiet that Lynne wondered if he and Jenny had slipped off to the pub. Then she heard noises upstairs. Filled with a sense of déjà vu, she began to climb up towards the bedroom. Once she was on the landing the sounds became louder, more identifiable. There was the dull thwack of something leather, followed by a low whimpering. Then came Jenny's sharp tone, full of sibilants, 'Sinners must be chastised! Say your prayers, you scurrilous sinner!'

Cautiously, Lynne opened the door and peeped in. There was Nick spread-eagled on the bed with some kind of black robe drawn up to expose his buttocks. Standing in fierce supremacy over him was Jenny, wearing, of all things, a grey nun's habit and wielding a thick leather strap. When Lynne saw the red stripes across her husband's buttocks she exclaimed aloud, 'My God, Jenny, what the hell do you think you're doing?'

Jenny turned and gave her a peculiar smile. At first she appeared sweetly angelic, but her eyes were cold and hard, chilling Lynne to the marrow. Nick turned his head and gave an equally strange abject grin, making Lynne recoil in horror. If this was their idea of an amusing sex game then she wanted no part of it.

Chapter Nine

ONCE AGAIN LYNNE found herself hovering in the doorway, unsure whether to go or stay. There was something horribly fascinating about the scene, with both Jenny and her husband now smiling complicitly at her. While she hesitated, Jenny put down the belt and came towards her, arms outstretched. She looked unnervingly pure and innocent with her hair tucked back behind her wimple, out of sight. 'Come in, Sister Linda,' she cooed.

'Look, I'm not into this,' Lynne protested, shrinking back.

Jenny took her hand. 'It's confession time, dear. Get down on your knees and Father Nicholas will hear you confess your sins.'

'That's right.' Nick had risen from the bed. He was wearing a cassock with a knotted cord at his waist and beneath the loose black gown his erection was very obvious.

'Look, you two . . .' she began, but then Jenny's grip on her wrist grew stronger.

'She is wilful, Father. She resists salvation. Help

me to win her for God.'

To Lynne's horror, the two of them overpowered her. They took off her jacket and forced her to kneel on the carpet. Nick whipped off his belt and bound her hands behind her back. She snapped at them angrily. 'For God's sake, you two, untie me! I told you, I'm not into this.'

'I think our sister is in need of correction, Father,' came Jenny's smoothly insinuating voice. 'She will not submit. We shall have to chastise her for the good of her soul.'

'Alas, I believe you are right, Sister Jennifer.'

He sat on the edge of the bed and, aided by Jenny, pulled his wife over his lap. Lynne struggled, but with hands tied there was little she could do. While Nick held her down, Jenny pulled up her skirt and pulled down her tights and knickers so her backside was exposed.

Lynne felt a shuddering horror at the prospect of a belting. So when she felt only the flat of Nick's hand slap her buttock she was relieved, despite her disgust at the whole business.

'That's right, Father,' she heard Jenny say.

As he began to slap her repeatedly, in a rhythmic fashion, the other woman kept up a running commentary. 'Beat it out of her, Father! Ooh, that's good! Make her squirm in the filth of her own sin . . . Aah! That's so good! And again, Father . . . Yes! Yes! Harder, Father, harder!'

Lynne's buttocks were stinging hotly now and her fury was intense, but it was obvious from the noises Jenny was making that she was getting off on seeing her spanked. Craning her neck round, Lynne could see that Jenny had her hand under her skirt and was rubbing herself frantically. Her face was red and she was panting loudly. As Lynne watched, she slowed her movements and threw her head back, moaning with ecstasy as her self-pleasuring reached its climax.

'Oh, that was divine, Father!' she murmured, gasping and sinking to her knees.

'But what of our sister?' Nick said. He'd stopped slapping Lynne's tender buttocks and was now stroking them gently. But her indignation still burned strong, and she was furious with the pair of them for taking advantage of her. 'We shall see if she will confess her sins.'

They allowed Lynne to sit on the bed, but they'd removed her shoes, tights and pants and her hands remained tied. She glared at them. 'I don't want any part of this silly game,' she declared, but they ignored her.

'Only confess, dear, and you shall know the rapture of divine love.' Jenny smiled sweetly. 'It has come to our ears that you shared a bed with two people last night, indulging in sins of the flesh. If you tell Father, in detail, what passed between you then he can absolve you.'

Lynne snorted, 'This is ridiculous!'

Nick frowned. 'She is obdurate, Sister Jennifer. I am afraid that we must resort to stronger measures to win her soul.'

Jenny picked up the leather belt and stroked it suggestively. 'I have the means, Father Nicholas.'

Remembering how she'd lambasted Nick, Lynne shuddered. 'You wouldn't dare! This is outrageous!'

'Who dares, wins!' Nick said with a grin. 'In this case, my dear, we win your eternal salvation. Is it not worth a little pain to enter the gates of heaven?'

'Let me go!'

'Only when you have confessed in full,' Jenny repeated.

Lynne gave an exasperated sigh. 'Look, this is becoming really tedious. It's Friday night and I have the weekend shopping to do. It's all right for you two to play your silly games but count me out, okay?'

'All we want is your confession, then you are free to go.'

Jenny looked from one to the other. They seemed equally determined to go through with the charade. Since she was bound and more or less helpless, she had no option but to do as they said and hope they would keep their word.

'Very well, I'll tell you about it. But I want you to know that I'm acting against my will. I'm only doing it so you'll untie me.'

'Of course,' Nick smiled. 'Put the belt away, Sister Jennifer. I don't think we shall be needing it after all.'

'What do you want to know?' Lynne asked sullenly.

Jenny grinned at Nick. 'Everything! In detail.'

'Well, I was with my husband and another woman. We were all naked. I was lying between them in the bed, and sometime in the middle of the night I was woken up by someone stroking my breasts and thighs.'

'Who was it?' Jenny asked eagerly.

'I'm not sure. It was dark. I think perhaps my husband was kissing my breasts and the woman was caressing my thighs.'

'Kissing?' Nick interjected sharply. 'You said stroking.'

'She began with her hands but then her lips took

over. My nipples were becoming really hard and tingling. My thighs were tingling too, from being massaged very gently. Soon my whole body felt tickly and warm.'

'Even your private parts?' Jenny asked, her voice hoarse with lust.

'Especially there.'

Despite her initial dislike of their scenario, Lynne found herself becoming aroused by the description of what had happened last night. It was obvious that the other two were in a similar state. They suggested she should lie down on the bed, to 'aid her memory', then they each lay beside her with their long robes hitched up.

Nick was slowly unbuttoning her blouse. 'Tell me, daughter, did you gain any pleasure from these sinful acts?'

'Some, Father.'

He pulled down her bra and exposed one rearing nipple, which hardened as he touched it. 'When your husband put his hand here, and stimulated you in this manner, did you feel any particular urges? Think carefully now, daughter.'

'Oh yes, Father. I certainly did.'

'And when the woman put her hand on your thigh did you long for her to place it higher up, to do some "tickling", perhaps?'

'I did.'

'Shame on you! Sister Jennifer, examine the woman at once. See if she is lasciviously aroused by this confession.'

Jenny parted her thighs and slowly drew her forefinger up the wet divide between the exposed labia. Lynne felt an exquisite pleasure as Nick pinched her nipple three times and Jenny poked the tip of her finger into her wet sex. But then the brief stimulation was ended, leaving her with an empty, aching desire for more.

'Oh yes, Father, she is certainly aroused. I think she needs to confess more of her sins before she is truly repentant.'

'Very well. Tell me, daughter, was your husband in a state of arousal while he was fondling your breasts?'

'I believe so. I could feel his erect member thrusting against my thigh.'

'Like this, perhaps?'

Nick rubbed his warm, fully erect penis against her, and she nodded. 'That's right. Exactly like that.'

'And what of the woman?' Jenny asked. 'Did she do any more to you?'

'Yes, she did. After a while I felt her move down the bed, under the duvet. She pulled my legs open and began to lick me, very thoroughly.'

'Really?' Lynne felt her shuffle down until her dark head was between her thighs. 'Like this, perhaps?'

As her swollen flesh was soothed by the rapid flickering of the invading tongue, Lynne forgot all her earlier misgivings. All she cared about now was to get her satisfaction, and she didn't much care what she had to do or say to achieve it. They had her dancing on the edge of an orgasm and she needed to come very badly now.

Nick's voice came, darkly insinuating, in her ear. 'You really are a very wicked girl, you know. Allowing yourself to be seduced by the pleasures of the flesh.' Lynne could tell that Jenny was rubbing his distended prick while she continued her enthusiastic cunnilingus. He seized his wife's breast where it jutted over her bra and licked her throbbing nipple between sentences, his beard hair tickling the sensitive surrounding skin. 'But now that you have confessed you shall receive blessings. Mm! Your blessed release from torment is assured . . .'

That release, when it arrived, came swift and strong, making Lynne writhe and moan with tumultuous gratification as her vagina convulsed repeatedly in time with her pulsating clitoris. She heard Nick groan and felt a warm stickiness against her thigh while Jenny's head came to rest between her knees.

Once the heat of Lynne's passion had faded, however, it was replaced by cold fury. She sat up, demanding that her hands be untied. Nick promptly obliged, but then she sprang up from the bed and stared down at the pair of them in their ridiculous robes. Her heart was thudding loudly, no longer from sexual arousal but from anger.

'You've both behaved despicably!' she snarled. 'I told you I wanted nothing to do with your sick fantasy, but you forced me into it.'

'Don't kid yourself, sister!' Nick grinned up at her. 'You enjoyed every minute of it, you know you did.'

'I certainly did not. If that's your idea of a good time then you're two very warped individuals, and I want nothing more to do with you.'

'Calm down, love,' Nick wheedled. 'We can talk about this later, if you like. Right now, I fancy a beer.'

'And I'd love some wine,' Jenny added.

Lynne stared at them incredulously. 'You really haven't got the message, have you? Well right now I'm going to change, and then I'm going to do my usual Friday night trip to the supermarket. Coming, Nick?'

'Er, maybe.'

'What's that supposed to mean?' Lynne snapped, as she found a clean pair of pants in the drawer. 'Are you coming or aren't you?'

'Well I think Jenny and I have some unfinished business. Can you wait an hour or so?'

He was giving her a beseeching look but Lynne wasn't fooled. She pulled on her jeans, then her socks and trainers. 'I know when I'm not wanted,' she said quietly. 'This whole business has been a sham, hasn't it? You didn't really want a threesome, either of you. All you wanted was to humiliate me with your stupid games. Well, it hasn't worked!'

'Lynne, it's not like that . . .'

Nick's protest fell on deaf ears as she left them to it and hurried downstairs. It was a relief to get out of the house and into her car, to speed off to the normality of familiar brands, special offers and checkouts. Yet as she pushed her trolley around the stacked aisles there was a numb ache around her heart. She felt hurt and betrayed. Not so much by Jenny, although she was annoyed with herself for being taken in by all those winsome smiles and girl-to-girl chats, but by her perfidious husband. He hadn't even had the guts to put the proposal to her himself but had let his mistress do it, knowing that she was capable of seducing his wife in the same way she'd seduced him. The whole thing stank to high heaven!

When Lynne returned to the house it was gone nine and from the faint sounds that filtered down from the bedroom she judged them to be still at it.

Well, sod them both! She turned on the portable television in the kitchen and put her dinner into the microwave. By the time the Friday evening episode of *Night Owls* came on they were still upstairs, so she settled down with a gooey dessert and did her best to enjoy the show.

It wasn't the same watching it by herself. Lynne felt cheated when she remembered how much she'd looked forward to the three of them watching together, maybe in bed, getting turned on by the scene where Blake got off with Sharna, an attractive Asian girl who was the latest of his conquests.

Despite knowing the plot in advance, Lynne was soon caught up in the drama. Carol only had a small part of the action, but she was pleased with the way she'd managed to convey her disapproval of Blake's womanising, and her annoyance at Penny's accusations that she was seeing Andrew behind her back.

When it came to the bedroom scene between Blake and Sharna, however, Lynne was struck by the stiltedness of the acting. There was a distinct lack of chemistry between the pair. Blake appeared to be going through the motions, while Sharna seemed scared stiff of him. Their dialogue was so unconvincing that Lynne was surprised Don had allowed it to go out. He must have been too worried about keeping on schedule to risk a re-take.

By contrast, the scene where Andrew had to confront Penny was quite riveting. Jonathan was pulling out all the stops, shouting and raving at his jealous screen girlfriend with a passion that he'd never shown before. Looking beyond the character he was acting, Lynne realised that the man had hidden depths. He'd always been pleasant and friendly to her. In fact she had come to rely more and more on his company between takes, yet she'd never suspected that strong passions might lurk beneath that quiet exterior. He'd begun to intrigue her.

After the programme ended there was still no sign of her husband and Jenny. Lynne ran a bath and lay soaking while she mused miserably about the future. She was sure the threesome wasn't going to work, but what followed from that? Would she and Nick be going ahead with the divorce after all? She'd believed there was hope for them, but if he'd rather play Jenny's perverted games than put serious effort into their marriage there was no point any more.

Still feeling depressed, Lynne went to bed alone in the spare room that night. Nick didn't bother to seek her out, presumably being too involved in their joint fantasy to care about her. She awoke next morning in a bad mood and more than ready to confront the pair of them with the set speech she'd been composing half the night. Stomping down to the kitchen she found Nick drinking coffee by himself.

'Where's Jenny?' she demanded. 'I've something to say, and I want to say it to both of you.'

His beard was more ragged than ever, making him look rakish. A pang of regret hit her.

Nick shrugged, smiling faintly. 'She's gone back to her flat. Thought it might be better if we had a chat by ourselves.'

'I see.' Grimly Lynne poured herself a coffee from the cafetière. 'Well I'm not surprised she couldn't face me.'

'It's not that. We're not ashamed of what we do together, Lynne. And if you're not into that particular game plan there are others. We're prepared to be flexible.'

Nick had put on his 'sweetly reasonable' tone, which only inflamed her anger. 'That's not the issue, Nick, and you know it! What I'm angry about is the way you and she totally ignored me when I said I wasn't into your horrible little play. You just wouldn't take no for an answer.'

'We both thought you were secretly enjoying it, honestly, Lynne.'

'That's always been the cry of the rapist, hasn't it?' she said scornfully. 'Look, I'm not against sex games in general. I've enjoyed that sort of thing before, you know I have. But it must be with the full consent of all parties. Seeing that woman whack you with a belt and bring up great weals on your backside was *not* my idea of fun. Neither did I want the same treatment myself. I thought you knew me better, Nick.'

'I'm sorry if you feel like that, but I can promise it won't happen again. Jen and I will save that sort of thing for when we're alone. I'm sure we can work out something else for the three of us to enjoy together.'

Lynne felt she was getting nowhere. She poured herself another coffee then said, 'I'm not sure I want that any more. For one thing I'd feel I was inhibiting you and Jenny, that you'd rather be doing other things. And I can't forget how you tied me up against my will. I'd always be afraid that you'd gang up on me again, and I wouldn't be able to relax enough to trust you. It just wouldn't work, Nick. The damage has been done.'

'So what are you saying?' He looked at her with weary, vulnerable eyes. For a moment she pitied him, longed to put her arms around him and say everything would be all right. But she no longer felt it was her place to do that. She might still be his wife, but Jenny had the hold over his darker, more passionate side and Lynne suspected she would always win in the end.

'I don't know,' she said, miserably. 'But I don't want Jenny round here again. If you want to see her you'll have to go to her place.'

'That's a real shame. I was hoping you two could be friends.'

'I don't hate her, Nick, don't think that. It's just that I can't be into what she seems to like doing. And if that's your bag, well I suppose I'll just have to get used to the idea.'

His face brightened. 'You mean you'll still let me live here, with you?'

'I'm prepared to try, if you are.'

'But you'll let me go on seeing Jenny?'

Nick looked as if it were too good to be true. Perhaps it was. Lynne had no way of assessing her feelings right then. 'Let's just put everything on hold, shall we? Until we all know what we want. At the moment I'm totally confused.'

He came to embrace her. She leaned her head against his chest with a sigh and he stroked her hair. 'Never mind, love. We'll get it sorted, don't you worry.'

They spent the rest of the weekend together in a state of marital harmony. The only trouble was that Lynne couldn't bring herself to make love with him. The spectre of Jenny and her weird ways intervened whenever her husband made an advance towards her, making her feel sickened. She just couldn't help it.

Once again it was a relief to escape to the fictional world of *Night Owls* on Monday morning. She congratulated Jonathan on his performance and he seemed delighted. 'I bet you never thought I had it in me, did you?' he grinned. 'I'm not just a pretty face, you know.'

No, you're certainly not, Jenny thought. In other circumstances she would have been interested in finding out more about his hidden depths, but right now she was too preoccupied with thoughts of Nick. She didn't want to lose him, yet she saw no way out of their dilemma.

Blake came up for the first time in ages and asked how she was. 'I'm fine,' she smiled brightly, but not very convincingly. He took her to one side, saying, in a conspiratorial whisper. 'Look, keep this under your hat, but a little bird told me there are some interesting developments afoot for our Carol.'

'Really?'

He put a finger to his lips. 'Mum's the word, though. Can't say more, but remember you heard it from me first!'

Lynne was cheered by the news. She'd been feeling increasingly fed up with the boring life that her character seemed to lead. Her own private life seemed incomparably more exciting!

That night Nick came home from work later than usual. He looked pale and drawn, so Lynne asked him what was the matter. Taking a beer out of the fridge he turned to face her. Lynne could tell he'd been drinking already, but she didn't say anything.

'I've decided that I only want you,' he declared, drinking straight from the bottle. 'So I told Jen it's over between us. Finished. From now on, sweetheart, it's just you and me.'

Lynne wished she could have given a more heartfelt response, but he looked so distressed it was hard to feel pleased. 'If that's truly what you want, Nick,' she said uncertainly.

He clung to her waist like a child, burying his face in her stomach. She ruffled his hair gently, wondering why she wasn't feeling overjoyed. He looked up at her with sad eyes.

'She didn't take it very well, Lynne.'

'No, I don't imagine she would.'

'I'm scared she'll do something silly. Let's put the answerphone on right away. I don't want her hurling abuse at you or anything.'

'Oh dear. That bad, was it?'

'She'll get over it. She just needs a bit of time. When we decided to try again I was so happy, Lynne. It was a stupid mistake to involve her. I should have made a clean break.'

'We were both fooled. I thought it might work too. I'd convinced myself we could all be best buddies.'

Nick laughed, and Lynne joined in. 'Let's go out and celebrate!' she suggested. 'Have a slap-up meal at that new Indonesian restaurant. I'd like that.'

The evening was a success. In a couple of hours Lynne learned to relax in Nick's company again, and when they returned home there was no unsettling message on the answerphone. They sat up listening to music they both enjoyed, and drinking brandy. Lynne almost managed to convince herself it was like the old days, and when Nick took her in his arms and kissed her with tender passion she felt ready to respond to him fully.

They made love in a pure and simple fashion that night, restoring Lynne's faith in their prospects. First Nick massaged her all over with some relaxing essential oil, then he stroked her pussy softly while he kissed her breasts until she was eager to make love, sighing and purring like a contented cat. He turned her over on to her stomach and came into her very slowly from behind so that by the time she raised her hips and began to wiggle her bum in the air he was in right up to the hilt. With one hand on her jutting clitoris and the other fondling each of her breasts in turn, Nick led her up to a sweet and gentle climax before coming himself. They sank down in each other's arms and Lynne was confident that at last they had dispelled the bad vibes that had lingered around their marital bed. She cuddled up, told him she loved him, and was soon asleep.

Two weeks passed happily, with no untoward repercussions from Jenny. Nick mentioned that she'd handed in her notice at work and was very obviously avoiding him, but that was all. No nasty phone messages were left, no poison pen letters, no angry confrontations at the door Lynne stopped thinking about her ex-rival, concentrating instead on re-building her relationship with her husband.

'You seem a lot happier lately, Lynne,' Jonathan commented one day at the studio.

'I am!' she replied, beaming. And it was the truth.

Then she had a week off from filming. Carol was supposed to be away, visiting a relative. Every soap actor and actress was entitled to a break once in a while – it was written into their contract – and now it was Lynne's turn. She would have liked to go away with Nick for a week's holiday, but he was too busy at work. Instead, he promised a trip to Brighton at the weekend. They were going to stay in the luxurious Metropole Hotel on Friday and Saturday nights, and Lynne was looking forward to it enormously.

Meanwhile, she decided to do some spring cleaning and re-decorate the bedroom. It was an important project to her, the final clearing away of unpleasant memories. She would paper the walls with something pretty, get rid of the carpet that she'd been forced to kneel on and 'confess her sins', change the curtains and the bed linen. For her it was almost an act of exorcism.

On Thursday afternoon she was happily working away dressed in faded, torn jeans and an old T-shirt with her hair done up in a scarf, when the doorbell rang. She put down her paintbrush and hurried downstairs calling, 'Just coming!' She flung open the door and saw a bald-headed man with a black moustache and wearing a trench-coat.

'Mrs Lynne Sanders?'

'Yes.'

'I wonder if I might have a few words with you. I'm Dan Fielding, from the *Echo*. I do have some identification . . .'

While he produced his card, Lynne felt her buoyant mood fade. What the hell did he want this time? 'Was it you who phoned me before?' she asked him, a sharp edge to her voice.

'Yes, but . . .'

'I thought I told you I didn't want to speak to you. I don't know why you're still bothering me. As far as I'm concerned that's over and done with.'

'Ah, but it's not about *that* business, Mrs Sanders. I've come about the recent news item which, I'm sure you'll agree, is a far more serious matter. We just thought you might like to put your side of the story.'

'What?' Amidst her confusion, warning bells were ringing loudly. 'What "news item"? What the hell are you talking about?'

'You mean you don't know?' He glanced round, as if anxious not to be overheard. 'It might be better if we talked indoors. I'm sure you wouldn't want any more bad publicity, especially on your own doorstep.'

Dazed, she let him in then led the way into the sitting room, where he plonked himself down in an armchair uninvited. Still standing she said, icily, 'Now would you mind telling me what this is all about?'

'See for yourself.'

He pulled a folded copy of 'Soaplines' from the inside pocket of his raincoat. Lynne's heart sank. Surely they were not going to put her through more trauma? The reporter opened it out and handed her the page. She saw a photo of her one screen kiss – a rather tame clinch with Blake – and then the headline: 'NIGHT OWLS' DO IT THREE IN A BED!

Instinctively she gasped, 'Jenny! The bitch!'

Lynne knew it could only be her who had leaked such a story. And that woman's only intention could have been to wound. Quickly she scanned through the rest of the article. There was some disgusting stuff about a 'love triangle' and her husband sharing his bed with his wife and mistress at the same time. The worst thing of all was that Lynne couldn't deny it.

'Perhaps you'd care to give me something printable,' the reporter said, smirking. 'We could run a denial story, but in my experience that's a waste of time. I'd advise you to go for the "jilted mistress" approach, if I were you. You know the sort of thing, "fabricating lies in spiteful revenge". If you like I could add something like, "she writes such good stories perhaps she should be taken on as a scriptwriter for *Night Owls*". Make light of it, that's your best bet.'

'Thanks for your advice,' she said, frostily, 'but I'd rather say nothing. It won't do any good. Once my husband hears about this he'll be devastated. It was bad enough last time.'

'Sorry!' The man shrugged. 'Personally I think hacks who produce that sort of filth should be hung, drawn and quartered. But since it's now in the public domain, and you live in our catchment area, I'm afraid I'm obliged to produce some sort of copy.'

'What will you write?' she asked faintly.

'Don't worry, I'll be as brief and tactful as possible. "No comment" always looks bad, so I'll have to say you're "devastated by the slur on your happy marriage" or something.'

'I never thought I'd have to put up with this sort of thing when I joined the cast of *Night Owls*,' Lynne sighed.

'That's good – very good. Can I quote you on that?'

Lynne gave a weary laugh. 'Oh, all right! Now, please, will you leave? I'm going to have to show this to my husband when he gets in. I'd rather he got it from me.'

For the next three hours Lynne waited in trepidation for Nick's return. She finished painting the woodwork then showered and washed her hair. She put on a clean pair of jeans and a sweatshirt, then made up her face. By the time she heard his key in the lock she had recovered some of her external composure, but inside she felt a total mess.

'Hi! How's the painting going?' He greeted her with a kiss. 'I thought I'd find you covered in pink splashes.'

'I had a shower. The woodwork's done. I opened the windows but it's still a bit smelly.'

What am I doing, talking domestic chit-chat? she asked herself. There was a hollow pain in her stomach, a griping apprehension that made her blurt out without any preamble, 'Nick, I've got some bad news. Jenny must have sold her story to that damn magazine . . .'

Nick's face bore an uncomprehending frown. 'Her story? What story?'

'About us. Look!'

She thrust the page at him and went to sit down, unable to watch him read it. In a few seconds he exploded. 'The little cow! I knew something was going on when she left so quickly. This is disgusting!'

Lynne shrank back as he towered over her, his face contorted with violent rage. 'How could you bring this on me? You've made me a laughing stock at work. It was bad enough trying to live it down the first time, but this is ten times worse!'

She thought she must have misheard him. 'I'm mad at her too, Nick. I trusted her, and I feel completely betrayed. I suppose she acted out of revenge.'

'Yes, but you gave her the opportunity.'

'I did *what*?'

'You heard. If you hadn't been in that bloody soap no-one would have been interested in your sex life, and this would never have happened.'

Lynne got to her feet. She was inwardly seething, but her voice was controlled ice.

'Nick, it sounds as if you're trying to blame *me* for what that woman has done.'

'Not all the blame, no. She shouldn't have

divulged those private details. But you shouldn't have antagonised her the way you did. You knew you were vulnerable to this sort of thing.'

Lynne felt her anger break free like a beast from its cage. 'You bastard! You're still on her side, even after what she's done to us! You're still trying to blame me, even though the whole thing was your idea. *I* never wanted anything to do with her. I thought if I went along with your plan I'd be able to keep you, but now I realise it was all a complete waste of time. You're a little shit, Nick. You like weird sex with weird women, and that's been the trouble all along. Well, you can sod off! Back to that bitch, if you like – you're well suited to each other. I'm going to re-open divorce proceedings first thing tomorrow!'

Chapter Ten

THE WEEKEND IN Brighton was now out of the question, much to Lynne's chagrin. She'd thought of going by herself, but someone was sure to recognise her. Once she would have proudly owned up to being 'Carol' from *Night Owls*, but things were different since 'Soaplines' had printed that dreadful article. She even put on a hat and dark glasses to go out shopping.

Her feelings about Nick were still bitter. He had moved out – where to Lynne neither knew nor cared. She was now convinced that their marriage was over, and on Sunday night she penned a note to her solicitor, asking her to resume divorce proceedings.

Lynne was also dreading going back to work. Although nothing had been said about her last appearance in 'Soaplines', this time she was sure it would be different. Jonathan had mentioned how annoyed Don had been over Blake's notoriety, and what had been said about her was far more salacious. Still, it couldn't be helped now.

Her misgivings were confirmed when she walked

into Sphere TV and was told Don wanted to see her right away. The cast were seldom summoned to the lion's den, so there was real cause for alarm. When Lynne entered, Rob Bates, the script editor, was with him.

Don greeted her with an outstretched hand and a warm smile. 'Ah, Lynne! Do take a seat.' She sank into a leather chair, mystified. 'We wanted to have a word with you about the direction that Carol's story will be taking,' Don went on, filling her with relief. 'We feel it's time to spice her up a bit. To be honest, she's been going nowhere. We had to have a barmaid, and we needed a foil for Andrew and Penny, but we hadn't thought much beyond that.'

'Well, I was getting a bit bored,' Lynne admitted with a cautious grin.

Rob said, 'If you're bored with her, the viewers will be too. So here's what we've come up with.' He handed her a few pages of script. 'Have a skim through that.'

The scene took place at Penny's flat. She'd asked Carol to come round for a chat, apologising for being jealous and wanting to make friends. As Lynne read on she was amazed to find that Penny was actually admitting to being jealous of Andrew, not Carol. Apparently the girl was bi-sexual, and really fancied the barmaid. The scene ended on a cliff-hanger: would Carol respond to Penny's advances or not?

'I'm amazed! What happens next?'

'To some extent that depends on you,' Rob said. 'We wouldn't want to spring a full-blown lesbian affair on your character unless you were prepared to go along with it. To be honest, we wouldn't normally change course like this. We like to have our characters fully worked out in advance. But Carol was brought into the show in a bit of a hurry, as you know.'

'What we want from you is some indication of how you'd like us to proceed,' Don explained. 'We have three options. Tell her, Rob.'

'Okay. We can either have her rebuff Penny outright, and that'll be the end of that, except that we might continue Penny's love-life with another character. Plan B would have Carol responding to some extent, with a bit of kissing and cuddling but no nudity. And the last option would be for them to have an out-and-out lesbian affair. Tastefully done, of course.'

Lynne's mind was buzzing. 'Can I think about it?'

Don smiled. 'Of course. You don't have to decide right now, Lynne, but we'd like a definite response by the end of the week, please.'

'I suppose you'd rather I agreed to go at least some of the way?'

'As Rob said, we intend to develop that side of Penny's character, if Sandra's willing, but it doesn't have to be with Carol. Homosexuality is a popular theme in soaps right now and since we go out after the watershed we could be a bit more raunchy. The audience research chaps tell us quite a few gays watch *Night Owls*. Blake is becoming a bit of an icon, it seems.'

'Blake?'

'Yes. He's bi-sexual, didn't you know? We're thinking of bringing in a toy-boy for Hugo, but that's strictly between us at the moment.' Don rose from his chair. 'Anyway, Lynne, take that script away and read it again at your leisure. Let us know as soon as possible, would you?'

As she shook hands with the two men, Lynne still felt bewildered. Don went to open the door for her, adding, in a low voice, 'If we do go ahead with the Sandra and Carol story the media publicity will be hot, but our viewing figures will benefit. I want you to understand that.'

On the way to make-up, Lynne pondered his words. After expecting the producer to give her a rocket for getting into the gutter press, he seemed to be suggesting it was good for business. But could she stand more of the kind of thing she'd already been through? Well at least she no longer had a marriage to protect, she told herself ruefully.

As for the news about Blake, she wasn't altogether surprised. It now made sense that he'd failed to follow through after his initial seduction of her.

Once again it was Jonathan who sensed her subdued mood when she appeared on set.

'I thought you'd come back full of the joys of spring after your week off,' he smiled. 'How did the weekend in Brighton go?'

She regretted having mentioned it, but she couldn't fob him off with a lie. 'It didn't, I'm afraid.'

He looked genuinely concerned. 'What happened?'

'Oh, I suppose it was unrealistic to imagine that it would be a second honeymoon. The fact is, Nick and I have split up again and this time it looks like for good.'

'I'm sorry. Look, Lynne, if you don't want to eat alone tonight I know a decent little place nearby. I was thinking of eating there anyway.'

'Thanks, Jon. I might just take you up on that.'

She was relieved he hadn't mentioned the 'Soaplines' article. Perhaps he didn't know yet.

With half her mind on other matters, Lynne gave a lack-lustre performance that day. At six-thirty, when she was leaving her dressing room, Jonathan reminded her of his invitation.

'Yes, I'd love to eat with you,' she smiled. Anything to put off the evil hour when she must return to an empty house.

The Italian restaurant was comfortable and quiet, almost empty that early in the evening. Lynne felt like opening up to Jonathan. She felt badly in need of a sympathetic ear.

'Did you see the latest edition of "Soaplines"?' she asked him.

'Yes, but I wasn't going to bring it up unless you did.'

'That's very tactful of you. As you might have guessed, that was more or less the last straw for my marriage.'

'Those scum never consider the consequences, do they? I suppose it's no consolation that you'll just be a nine-day wonder then fade from the spotlight.'

'I'm not so sure about that. Look, I shouldn't be telling you this, Jon, but I know you'll be discreet.' She glanced over her shoulder to ensure there was no-one within earshot before continuing in a low voice. 'Don wants Carol to have a lesbian affair with Penny.'

'No! Really? Good grief!'

He began to chuckle, and Lynne found his laugh infectious. She giggled until the tears flowed. It was a welcome release of the tension that had been building in her all weekend.

'Another case of art imitating life!' Jonathan grew serious. 'But how do you feel about that, Lynne? I mean, people are bound to see it as confirming the rumours about your private life.'

She shrugged. 'My private life's in ruins anyway now, so what does it matter?'

'Is that true? Is there no hope of you patching things up with your husband?'

She shook her head. 'The woman he left me for was the one who sold that story to "Soaplines". Basically, he sided with her against me.'

'How could he? I'm so sorry, Lynne.'

'But let's not talk about such gloomy topics. I'd rather forget about my own dismal life. Tell me about yourself, Jon. I know so little about you. Where were you brought up? How did you first get into acting?'

She learned that he had taken a degree in Psychology before going into rep and making his way first in the theatre, then in television. Lynne found she could remember the TV commercials he'd done – especially one for throat sweets, where he played the front end of a hoarse pantomime horse!

They chatted happily for a couple of hours and the restaurant filled up around them. When it was obvious that their table was needed for another couple, they paid the bill and left. Lynne felt happy and more relaxed than she had for ages.

'Can I give you a lift anywhere?' Jonathan asked as they reached the Sphere car park.

'Well, I live in Ealing, and normally I use the Underground . . .'

'No problem,' he grinned. 'My place is in Richmond, practically en route.'

Richmond. The name gave Lynne a sad twinge. How far away that golden afternoon with Nick now seemed, full of false hope and doomed passion!

In the warm intimacy of Jonathan's small car,

Lynne felt completely at ease. He drove quite slowly and they continued their conversation in a rambling way, discovering a mutual love of certain actors, authors and musicians. Somehow she and Nick had never quite shared the same tastes, except for a couple of classical composers they'd both liked.

Inevitably she began to feel drawn to him in a physical as well as an emotional way. She couldn't help looking at his strong square hands, and noticing the clean cut of his jawline in profile. His good looks were understated, but all the more effective when you took a closer look. She began to wonder if he had a steady girlfriend: if so, he wasn't mentioning her. Despite her recent heartache, Lynne's hopes began to rise again. There *were* decent, kind, sexy, eligible men still left in the world and one was sitting next to her right now!

When he drew up outside her door Lynne wrestled with her conscience. Should she invite him in? While she hesitated, he leaned across and touched her cheek. 'Lynne, thanks for spending the evening with me,' he smiled. 'I didn't want to go home to an empty flat either.'

She looked into his blue eyes, with their questioning expression, and her stomach flipped. He lifted her chin with his forefinger and softly pressed the moist cushion of his mouth against her half open lips. Lynne opened her mouth wider, their tongues making tentative contact. She ran hers along the top of his bottom lip, tempting him in, and soon he was thrusting deep inside, meeting her halfway, with his hands clutching her shoulders and upper arms.

Lynne could feel her body tuning up for more, a slow vortex gathering strength within. She knew that her breasts were taut and stiff-nippled and her pussy was already wet, and that if he kissed her for much longer she couldn't resist him. But then he withdrew, first his tongue, then his lips and finally his hands. Dazed, she attempted to smile at him and it took her a few seconds to realise what he was saying.

'Well, goodnight, Lynne. See you in the morning.'

She could have asked him in even then, but something about his manner suggested he might refuse and she couldn't bear that. Completing her weak smile, Lynne muttered her thanks and got out of his car. She waved as he drove off but was nevertheless filled with sadness. Probably he did have a girlfriend. It was hardly likely that a good-looking and sweet guy like that would be unattached.

Somehow Lynne got through the night and was up in time for work next day. Spending the evening with Jonathan had helped her to forget her troubles for a while, and today she felt more optimistic. When she got into the studio, however, he was deep in conversation with Sandra, who played Penny. Lynne watched the actress with more than passing interest, knowing that she was scheduled to work with her in a way that could be quite embarrassing if she didn't feel comfortable about it.

It was only when she saw the two of them together, heads almost touching, that it suddenly dawned on Lynne that there could be something going on between them. It hadn't occurred to her before. When Jonathan had mentioned Sandra it had been only as a colleague, but now she saw them in a new light. Sandra's eyes were sparkling as they shared a joke, and Jonathan gave her a brief touch on the arm before turning to walk away.

He caught sight of Lynne and came over. 'Hi! How d'you feel today?'

'All the better for seeing you last night,' she answered, keeping her voice down. Over his shoulder she could see Sandra's inquisitive, slightly apprehensive expression.

'Good. We must do it again sometime.'

Then the call came to start filming, and Lynne began mentally rehearsing her lines.

She hoped to see Jonathan again at lunch time, but Blake told her he'd gone over the road to the pub. 'That's where I'm off to,' he added. 'Coming?'

Lynne nodded. When the two of them were in one of the deserted corridors, Blake suddenly turned to her with a grin. 'I gather you've been told about the little surprise in store for Carol,' he said. 'Well, was I right, or was I right?'

'You certainly were! But I still haven't made up my mind if I can handle it.'

'Well, by all accounts you've had some practice in that department!'

Lynne was stunned. A cold anger filled her, and she rushed forward but Blake caught her arm. 'Don't take offence, Lynne, there was no harm meant. You've got to laugh at the gossip columns, make light of it. That's the only way, believe me.'

'Yes, you've given them plenty of good copy too, haven't you?' she answered bitchily. It gave her some relief to take it out on him.

But he wasn't thrown. 'Most of us have, at some time or other. It's the price of fame. But seriously, Lynne, if you want to do some research for the part I know just the place – this club I belong to. You could come along as my guest one evening, if you like. No-one will bother you, I promise. And you might find it helps you make up your mind.'

She stared at him, half tempted by his offer. 'Maybe. I'll think about it.'

'You do that. It takes all sorts, you know, Lynne. And if you want to be a really good actress you need to live a little, go people-watching, find out how the rest of us get along.'

'I'm sure you're right. I'm just not sure I'm ready for it yet.'

They went over to the pub, which was noisy and smoky as usual. While Blake bought her a drink, Lynne looked around. Suddenly she caught sight of Jonathan and was about to give him a wave when she realised he was with Sandra. They were talking in a way that excluded others, and he was holding her hand. Filled with disappointment, Lynne took her drink from Blake and followed him to a free table at the opposite end of the pub.

'Cheers! Here's to Carol and Penny!' Blake grinned, downing his beer.

Lynne saw Jonathan out of the corner of her eye. He was looking in their direction. Something made her lean closer to Blake, smile and say, 'You know, I think I will take up that offer of yours. To come to your club, I mean.'

'Really?' Blake beamed, his lazy eyes flashing wide for a few seconds. He patted her hand. 'Excellent. You won't regret it, it's the best club in town. How about this Friday?'

'Okay.'

Just before two, Lynne rose with Blake. Jonathan and Sandra were also moving out, and they all coincided at the door. 'Come on, you two lovebirds,' Blake said ironically. 'Kiss and make up, why don't you?'

'We already have!' Sandra laughed. 'Didn't you see this morning's scene?'

'Too busy learning my lines for this afternoon!'

Lynne tried to join in, to share the joke with Jonathan by smiling or winking at him, but he deliberately averted his eyes and she felt snubbed. It hurt to have him ignore her. In the scene that afternoon, Andrew had to come into the bar and have a brief exchange with Carol. Jonathan went through the motions, but the usual spark was missing.

Lynne felt guilty. Had she flirted with Blake too much in the pub? But Jonathan had been tête-à-tête with Sandra. Besides, neither had any claim on the other. Last night's kiss could have been an attempt to cheer her up on his part, nothing more. She'd been foolish to imagine he thought of her as anything more than a friend and colleague.

On Friday morning Don reminded her that she had until Monday to make up her mind about Carol's future. 'Makes you feel kind of godlike, doesn't it?' he grinned. 'Having your character's fate in your hands, I mean. Don't let the rest know, though, or they'll all be wanting to run the show!'

Lynne didn't like to tell him that at least two of the cast knew already.

Blake said he would pick her up at nine that evening to take her to the club, which was situated in Chiswick. He wasn't very helpful when she asked him what she should wear, shrugging his shoulders and saying 'Anything goes, anything at all!' In the end she decided to look as extrovert as possible and chose a pink chiffon blouse tied under her black lace bra, black leggings and dangly silver earrings.

She could almost her her mother exclaiming,

'Good Lord, Lynnette, you're not going out dressed like *that*!' But then she could hear her father's gentler voice saying, 'Let the girl wear what she likes, Eileen. She's only young once!' The memory brought tears to her eyes. She'd badly needed her dad's support in her late teens, but he had been no longer there for her.

Lynne waited for Blake's car in a mood of faint defiance. Tonight she was going to be notorious for a change! If people recognised her and sniggered, what did she care? Let them think what they liked. At least she would have Blake to protect her.

But when he arrived his appearance shocked her. 'Blake! You're wearing make-up!'

'So are you,' he grinned, giving her a brief kiss on the cheek. 'How appropriate, since we're both in the acting profession!'

Even so, it wasn't discreet make-up. Lynne thought she'd gone to town with the eye-liner and false lashes, but she had nothing on Blake. Great swathes of iridescent turquoise and purple adorned his heavy lids, making him look like some exotically painted lizard. She couldn't see what he was wearing beneath his enveloping black cape, but her mind boggled.

On the way, he told her more about where they were going. 'It's mainly a gay club, but Fridays and Saturdays are open nights. You'll find all genders there tonight, I can assure you.'

'*All* genders?'

'Mm. The usual two, plus men who used to be women and vice-versa, men dressed as women and vice-versa, and plenty who aren't quite sure what they are.'

'I'm not sure I'm ready for this.'

Blake patted her hand with his ring-decked fingers. 'Don't worry, it's all in the best possible taste! And no-one will make unwelcome advances to you, I can promise you that.'

At the door, a man in a black leather catsuit greeted Blake with a kiss on the cheek then turned his curious eyes on Lynne asking, 'Has he given you the rundown on this place, sugar?' She nodded. 'Good. In you go then. Party on, dudes!'

Inside, the flashing lights and loud music assaulted Lynne's eyes and ears. Blake handed his cloak to the attendant with a flourish and revealed a pair of skin-tight black leather trousers, topped by an elaborate Indian T-shirt decorated with mirror glass and sequins.

'Wow, you look great, Blake darling!'

Lynne turned to see a tall 'she-male' approaching, immaculately dressed in an evening gown, only his deep voice giving him away.

'Virginia! Darling!' Blake embraced his friend then introduced Lynne.

'Ooh, it's "Carol" the barmaid, isn't it? What a treat to meet you, gorgeous!' He lifted her hand and kissed it reverently. 'I watch every episode on video. It's recording now, even as I speak. Hi, Danielle! Hi, Suzi! Excuse me, darlings. Like blood, I have to keep circulating or I die, I just die!'

Blake gave Lynne a wink as Virginia sashayed on through the crowd. 'He's quite a character,' she grinned.

'Look, one point of etiquette, sweetheart. Here we refer to everyone as they appear to be, so Virginia's a "she", okay?'

'Oops, sorry! Thanks for telling me.'

'No harm done. Come and meet my dear friends

over by the bar. They have wonderful cocktails here, by the way.'

After Lynne had been introduced to an apparently straight couple called Alvin and Zoe, and been given a monstrous concoction called a 'Wet Dream' which bristled with rude cocktail sticks, they managed to find a corner table.

Blake put his arm around her shoulder. 'I'm going to leave you here for a while, Lynne dear. Don't worry, I'm sure nothing terrible will happen to you!' He turned to his friends, adding, in a stage whisper, 'She was a bit nervous about coming here, poor love. Not used to all this high living!'

'We'll look after her, Blake,' Zoe promised, with a smile.

'While they chatted, Lynne stirred her drink with a miniature plastic penis and examined her companions. Alvin had a mop of fair hair and a droopy yellow moustache. He wore a fringed suede jacket and James Dean T-shirt, with jeans. Zoe wore a pink nylon top, sleeveless with a roll neck, leopard skin hot pants and thigh-length black boots. Her clothing accentuated the size of her shapely breasts and the length of her thighs. She was very pretty in a stereotypical way, with large brown eyes and back-combed hair that formed an appealing halo to her pale face. Somehow, Lynne felt relaxed in their company and began to open up.

Then came the topic she'd dreaded. Zoe said, 'From that article in "Soaplines" I'd have thought you often went to clubs like this, Lynne.'

Seeing her embarrassment, Alvin came to her rescue. 'That just shows you shouldn't believe all you read in the papers, doesn't it?'

'I think everyone's entitled to a private life,'

Lynne said.

Zoe smiled. 'Absolutely! But once you go public, you're fair game. Everyone knows that. Look what they did to Blake!' Lynne couldn't resist following her gaze to the dance floor where the man himself could be seen with his arm round a glamorous transvestite's waist. 'In his case, though, he courts publicity. Thrives on it!'

'Pardon me saying so,' Alvin broke in, 'but I think that character you play, Carol, is a bit of a nonentity. Don't get me wrong, I think you play the part very well. It's just that nothing much seems to happen to her, does it?'

Lynne couldn't help laughing. 'Watch this space! You'll soon be eating your words.'

Zoe leaned forward eagerly, her brown eyes gleaming. 'Really? Can you give us a clue or are you under strict orders not to divulge the plot?'

Lynne knew she shouldn't rise to the bait, but the cocktail was bubbling up inside her, loosening her tongue. 'I'm not supposed to say anything, but I will give you a clue. Something may happen between her and Penny.'

'Not a torrid lesbian affair!' Alvin chortled.

Lynne knew she'd said too much, and cursed her 'Wet Dream'. She put a finger to her lips. 'Nothing's been decided yet.'

Zoe leaned back in her chair and thrust out her breasts, the erect tips of her nipples clearly outlined beneath the pink nylon. She had a thoughtful look on her face, and Lynne had the uneasy feeling that there was some hidden agenda forming behind those big brown eyes.

The music became more upbeat and Alvin said, 'Hey, why don't we dance?'

Zoe took her hand to help her to her feet and the three of them joined the throng. Lynne suddenly felt like an extra on a 'Star Trek' set – everyone looked as if they hailed from another planet. Yet there was a very warm and pleasant vibe going round.

Blake had been right – it was the best club in town. Lynne felt she was shaking her troubles away as she swayed in time to the music, mesmerised by the pulsing light show. Everyone seemed high on something, and there was a highly-charged atmosphere of eroticism. Raw sex was all around her. She could smell it in the heavy perfumes that the transvestites wore to give them the borrowed scent of a woman. She could see it in the flirty looks that were criss-crossing over the dance floor, like the courting signals of exotic birds, and in the shaking breasts and snaking hips that made up their mating dance. She could hear it in the heavy breathings, sighs and whispers that filled the air. She could feel it in the smooth-skinned arms and legs that brushed against her, the hands that pressed lightly on her bottom or touched her shoulder in passing. Even her taste buds were activated as she glugged down the spritzy water with a hint of juice that Zoe gave her to stop her drying out. It made her mouth clean and fresh, eager for new sensation.

Lynne didn't know how long she'd been dancing. She was in a timeless world of pure energy, and only when Zoe tapped her on the arm and whispered, 'I'm going to chill out for a bit, coming?' did she realise that she needed to rest her weary body.

She followed her small, trim figure through a bead curtain and into a corridor with several curtained booths. One of them had the curtain drawn aside and was obviously empty. It was lit by a low lamp and there was a couch scattered with cushions. A carafe of mineral water and a box of tissues stood on a small cupboard, and there were erotic Indian prints on the wall. Lynne flopped on to the sofa while Zoe pulled the curtain across then came over with a smile.

'Whew!' she exclaimed, sitting down beside her. 'Sometimes you forget how hot and dehydrated you can get.' She pulled off her pink top and revealed her naked breasts. They were perfectly round and pert, with large, erect nipples. Hastily Lynne averted her eyes.

'Have some water.' Zoe poured two glasses and handed Lynne one. There was faint, ambient music playing from a hidden speaker, relaxing and quiet. Now that the alcohol-enhanced high of dancing had faded Lynne was aware of a different, but related, excitement. She had a secret desire to reach out and touch those provocative breasts, but she didn't know whether Zoe wanted her to or not.

'What's Sandra Woods like?' Zoe enquired, out of the blue.

'You mean, the actress who plays Penny?' Zoe nodded. 'I don't know her all that well. We've talked a bit about how our characters should interact, of course.'

Zoe laughed. 'I should imagine you'll have a few more conversations like that if Carol has an affair with Penny!'

'Look, it's not decided yet. I shouldn't have said anything, really, so I hope you won't spread it around.'

'I promise, but it'll be great if it comes off. I mean,

so many women are making love with other women these days, whether they're exclusively lesbian or like me.'

'Like you?'

'I'm attracted to both men and women.' She smiled, and Lynne's pulse accelerated. She wasn't used to feeling desire for another woman but since the episode with Jenny she realised that she had the potential to be bi-sexual too.

Zoe leaned forward, her breasts swinging like bells. 'And I'm attracted to you, Lynne. When I read that you had shared your husband with another woman I thought "Good for her!" That takes real guts.'

Her brown eyes were surveying Lynne, assessing her interest. She must have been encouraged because she put Lynne's hand to her own breast, saying softly, 'Stroke me, please.'

Soon they were kissing, Zoe's fingers untying the knot of her blouse. Their tongues met, and Lynne groaned as the other woman found her way into the black bra and began to circle her stiff nipples with her thumbs. She could feel the heat in her crotch and the first hint of dampness as her clitoris tingled and swelled. Beneath her own fingers Zoe's taut breasts felt warm and smooth, their full curves heavy as they brushed against her palms.

Quickly Zoe undid her bra, freeing her from its frustrating constraint, then she bent to suckle on each clamouring nipple in turn. Her hands moved down to the waistband of Lynne's leggings and she began to roll down the garment, exposing the scrap of lace that covered her pubis. Her fingers snaked in amongst the matted hair and Lynne opened her thighs to give her access, sighing with relief as she felt the first direct contact with her hardened clitoris.

With her other hand Zoe leaned over and opened the door of the cupboard. She took out something with a harness attached. Lynne watched in amazement as the other woman got out of her hot pants, stripped off her miniscule knickers and strapped on the device. It was double-ended and reared between them like a huge pink banana.

'Ever been screwed by a woman?'

'Er . . . no. And I'm not at all sure about this.'

Zoe grinned. 'Don't worry. Just close your eyes and think of . . . well, anything you like!'

Lynne still felt doubtful, but when Zoe's finger slipped gently inside her, to check out if she was ready for her, it was obvious to both of them that she was quite turned on by the idea. Lynne watched as one end of the dildo disappeared into Zoe's well-primed vagina, then felt the other end ease its way into her own. At once her walls gripped the alien invader and she felt her clitoris twitch with impatient longing. As Zoe flicked the switch that set the vibrator humming and began to gently thrust in and out Lynne closed her eyes and sighed with pleased recognition. The effect was remarkably like being pleasured by a real, live man.

With Zoe's hands stroking her bottom and thighs, Lynne managed to get into a steady rhythm, lifting her hips in time with the stimulating back and forth motion. A sensual heat spread through her body and it wasn't long before the image of Jonathan Miles floated into her mind. Whether it was the association with Sandra or the memory of his good night kiss she didn't know, but once he arrived he was there to stay. She imagined that it was his hands gently caressing her, his penis that was slowly bringing her arousal towards its peak, his body that was erotically tuned into hers, making the experience one of mutual gratification.

Confident now that she wouldn't lose contact with the pulsating device, Lynne began to move her hips faster, abandoning herself to the thrilling currents that were swirling inside her. Zoe was rubbing the top of her vulva now, massaging the area around her clitoris where the vibrator couldn't reach, and Lynne's reactions sharpened, hastening the approach of her orgasm. She gasped as the tension rose, and heard answering moans as the pace speeded up once more. Remembering the passion that Jonathan had shown towards Sandra in his screen persona, she imagined him making those powerful thrusts into her hot interior, seeking her satisfaction as keenly as he sought his own. Most of all, she was imagining that he loved her.

The thought of his whispered words of love finally pushed her over the edge into the ecstatic free-fall of her climax. Once again she knew that sense of warm reassurance, enabling her to let go completely and give herself up to the oncoming waves of pure sensual delight. It was only when the pulse of her orgasm began to slow and then to fade that she came out of her dream and realised that her rapture had been induced by a woman with an electronic dildo. Then she was overcome by a sense of self-disgust and she felt horribly cheated.

Recognising that it wasn't Zoe's fault, she cuddled up to the other woman on the couch and said how much she'd enjoyed it, but inside there was a bleak emptiness which made her long to get away from that person and that place, to be alone with her feelings. After a while, Zoe began to put her clothes back on.

'Maybe that'll make it easier for you to do those lesbian love scenes on TV,' she smiled. 'I'll look forward to seeing them.'

Lynne gave a wry, sad smile. 'Maybe. I'm making no predictions.'

Zoe gave her a deep, affectionate kiss. 'Well, all I can say is that Sandra is a lucky girl! You're quite something, Lynne.' She opened her purse and took out a card. 'Look, here's my phone number. Call me soon, won't you?'

Lynne said she would but privately doubted it. As far as she was concerned this had been unrepeatable, and in the world that Blake, Zoe and Alvin inhabited she had a feeling that such a one-off encounter was par for the course. Not wanting to disturb Blake, who was well in with a crowd near the bar, Lynne told Zoe she was taking a taxi home.

'Are you sure?' she asked, anxiously. 'I could give you a lift if you like.'

'No, you stay,' Lynne said firmly. 'You're more used to this scene than I am.'

'But you did enjoy it, didn't you? I mean, you're not upset or anything?'

Lynne kissed her cheek. 'Not at all! I'm just worn out, that's all. Say my goodbyes to Blake, please, and thanks for making my evening worthwhile.'

Zoe gave her a wistful smile, and Lynne had the feeling that she would have liked to prolong not only the evening but the relationship, yet she knew in her heart that it wasn't on.

'See you around!' Lynne smiled, then went to phone for a taxi.

Chapter Eleven

LYNNE DECIDED TO compromise. She told Don that she was prepared to do a single love scene with Sandra, after which Carol would decide that lesbianism wasn't for her and Penny would have to look elsewhere. After all, she had no desire to be typecast as a gay actress. A week later Rob called a meeting of Sandra, Lynne and Jonathan.

'Initially, Andrew will know nothing about his girlfriend's seduction of Carol,' he explained. When he does find out he'll break off the relationship. It's been on the rocks for some time, as you know.'

'What about Carol?' Lynne wanted to know. 'I mean, what's her motivation for going along with Penny?'

'Well, she hasn't had a boyfriend for a while, and she's a bit confused about her own sexual orientation.'

'Hey, that's a bit sudden isn't it?' Jonathan frowned. 'I mean, how are you going to get that across to the viewers?'

'She's going to have a heart-to-heart with Hugo. As you know, we're building up his bi-sexual image too, so it will come up quite naturally.'

'And what will happen to poor old Andrew after all this?'

Rob grinned. 'Let's take this one step at a time, shall we? You know we don't like to give too much away. But take it from me that there's something pretty good on the horizon for him, once he's got shot of Penny.'

After the meeting Lynne was not much the wiser. She would have to wait to see the script, but meanwhile she had a few days off.

'What are you going to do with your free time?' Jonathan asked her as they sat in the coffee lounge afterwards.

She shrugged. 'Oh, I don't know. Maybe catch up on some reading, letter writing.'

Lynne had been avoiding Jonathan since she saw him in the pub with Sandra. Despite her undoubted attraction to him she didn't want any more heartache. Yet now he seemed to want to be friends again.

'I have a couple of days off too,' he told her. 'And I wondered if you'd like a day out in Brighton. I know you were disappointed when your weekend had to be called off. We could easily get there by train.'

She looked at him, trying to estimate what was going on in his mind. Was he just being matey, or was there more to it? And what about Sandra? For a moment she was inclined to refuse, but then she realised that it was a long time since she'd been out of London and the weather had been very pleasant lately. It would undoubtedly do her good to have a break. Besides, she'd been missing his company. Right now, she felt she needed all the friends she could get.

'That would be nice,' she smiled.

'Good. Shall we make it next Wednesday, then?'

Lynne still had misgivings about spending the day with Jonathan. Remembering how she'd fantasised about him, how close they'd been, she couldn't help wondering if she was inviting more heartbreak. She almost called it off at the last minute, but the weather seduced her. It was so perfectly warm and sunny, so perfect for a day at the seaside, that she couldn't resist it. They met at Victoria station and took the non-stop train. As she came out of Brighton station and began to walk down the hill towards the blue horizon, Lynne was suddenly overcome by a pang of nostalgia.

'Oh God, I remember Dad bringing me here, when I was about thirteen!' she exclaimed, her eyes brimming with tears.

Jonathan took her arm, sensing her mood. 'Was that the last time you were here?' he asked softly. She nodded, unable to speak. He put his arm around her and gave her a comforting hug. 'Don't be sad, Lynne. Try to remember the good times.'

She took out a tissue and blew her nose. 'Yes, it was a good day,' she sighed. 'I remember us going on the pier and walking up to Black Rock, where we explored the rock pools. It's the last clear memory I have of my dad.'

They walked on down to the sea front, where they found a café. Lynne was still lost in the past, scarcely aware of Jonathan's presence until he jolted her out of her dreams and memories.

'Lynne, have you ever tried to find your father?'

'What?'

'I wondered if you'd thought of tracing him. I mean, it wasn't all that long ago that he went away, was it?'

'I tried for a while after he left, but got nowhere. Now I wouldn't know where to start.'

'Your mother has no idea?'

'No, she didn't want to have anything more to do with him.'

'What about his relatives?'

'He was an only child, and both his parents were dead by the time he left home. You know, Jonathan, when I got the part in *Night Owls* I really hoped that he might watch it and try to get in touch, but it hasn't happened.'

'It still might.'

Lynne frowned, finishing her coffee. 'I don't even know if he's still in this country. Come on, let's go down to the beach. I'm dying to walk on those pebbles again!'

Despite the underlying sadness of the day, Lynne was determined to have a good time. They wandered round the Lanes, looking at the antique shops, then had lunch in the Metropole, which she insisted on out of a perverse desire to recreate some of the time she would have spent there with Nick. Jonathan understood. In fact, he was turning out to be the most understanding man she'd ever known. If only she could think of him as just a friend everything would be fine.

But later, as she lay on the beach in her bikini, Lynne found herself eyeing his semi-nude body from behind her sunglasses and silently cursing Sandra Woods. She felt horribly jealous as she looked at that well-developed chest, those broad shoulders and strong thighs. A reckless mood was creeping up on her, a wicked voice saying 'What the hell if he does have a girlfriend? He's with you now!' She could only hold it in check by recalling all the heartache she'd been through when Jenny had stolen her man.

When Jonathan rolled over and asked her to rub suntan lotion into his back, she wondered how she could bear to touch him. His skin felt so wonderfully smooth and warm beneath her fingers. She wanted to press her naked breasts against that broad expanse, to snuggle up with her pelvis pressed against those firm, shapely buttocks.

But it was even worse when Jonathan suggested he should return the favour. She lay face down, with her bikini top undone, his hands moved lovingly over her shoulders and down her sides, where they could brush lightly against the swell of her breasts. Her bikini pants were low-cut and the tip of his finger probed tantalisingly beneath them for a few seconds, making her squirm. Then he started on her legs, his thumbs so perilously close to the danger area as he spread the oil slick up her inner thighs. Pressing her pubis hard into the pebbles, Lynne could feel the juices seeping out of her and knew that he must have realised how aroused she was becoming. Perhaps he was doing it on purpose, the swine!

She cooled off later with a dip in the sea, but the attraction was still there. So much so that she hardly dared look at him, and when he took her hand to help her up the pebbly slope of the beach her entire body responded to his touch with tremulous intensity.

This is crazy, she told herself. I'm feeling like a love-struck teenager!

Yet it was impossible to imagine that he was not feeling the same. He kept hold of her hand as they walked along the prom and onto the pier. When she did risk looking at him the expression in his eyes was one of joyful pleasure in her company. They bought ice-creams and sat down to eat them, and he casually put his arm around her, drawing her close.

There were few people around, but Jonathan lowered his voice all the same as he asked, 'How do you feel about doing that love-scene with Sandra? I must say I think it's very brave of you to even attempt it.'

'It's not going to be easy,' she admitted. 'But I told Don I'm only prepared to go so far.'

'Of course it'll be easier for her.'

'Why? Has she done that sort of thing before?'

To her surprise, he laughed heartily. 'Oh Lord, didn't you know?'

'Know what?'

'She *is* a lesbian. I thought you knew that.'

Lynne broke into giggles, as much from relief as anything. So she'd been wrong about those two! The corresponding thought that the field was now clear for her and Jonathan made her throw her arms spontaneously around the man and kiss him. He responded passionately, and soon they were locked in a lovers' world of mutual desire and mounting hunger.

'Oh Lynne, I was afraid you'd gone off me!' he confessed.

She felt a fool. Somehow she couldn't bring herself to tell him the truth. 'Well, I was upset about my marriage. I still am, Jon. But that doesn't mean I don't value you as a friend.'

'Only as a friend?' he asked wistfully. His blue eyes were looking so appealingly at her that she couldn't resist teasing him a bit more.

'Well, let's say a very *close* friend!'

'How close?' He sidled up and took her firmly into his arms. 'This close?'

'Mm.'

His hands slipped under her top to find the bare skin of her midriff. 'This close?' he whispered.

'Mm!'

'Well, I'd like to get even closer. Do you think there's a chance of that?'

He nibbled tenderly at her earlobe while she assured him there was every chance of that.

As they walked off the pier, someone suddenly shouted, 'Hey, look! It's those two from that TV show!'

'Oh no!' Lynne groaned, but Jonathan smiled and waved at the gawking trio of holidaymakers. One came up and asked for autographs, then the others followed.

'You want to get rid of that Penny,' the woman advised Jonathan, in all seriousness. 'She's giving you the run-around.'

Lynne giggled. Little did they know what was in store! The woman continued, undaunted, 'And you, my dear, should get yourself a boyfriend. He'd do nicely, he would.'

'I'll do my best,' she replied, struggling to keep a straight face.

'It was too much to expect that we'd go completely unrecognised, even with dark glasses on,' Jonathan grinned as they crossed the road. 'Still, I reckon we got off lightly.'

They went back to the Metropole for dinner, at Jonathan's insistence. Halfway through the meal he said, on impulse, 'Why don't we stay the night?'

'What? Are you joking? It costs an arm and a leg.'

He took her hand. 'Don't you think we're worth it?'

'I suppose so, but . . .'

'But what? I'm paying.'

'I can't let you, Jon.'

'What's a couple of hundred quid for a night with the girl of my dreams?'

Lynne struck a romantic pose with her hand beneath her chin. 'Oh, you do say the sweetest things!'

'So have I persuaded you?'

She smiled. 'Looks like I'm going to get my dirty weekend in Brighton after all!'

But he suddenly turned serious. 'It's not dirty, Lynne. Neither is it only a bit of fun. I've wanted you for a long time, and I think I know you well enough to be sure this is not just a flash in the pan. So if you've got cold feet and want to back out now, just tell me and we'll go back to London.'

His words scared her a little, but she knew he was echoing her own heartfelt thoughts. She leaned over and kissed his lips. 'I want to stay here with you.'

Lynne had fantasised about her Brighton weekend with Nick, imagining a night of unfettered passion, but she was now sure it would be surpassed with Jonathan. As they walked into the bedroom she felt a warm thrill of anticipation, tinged with lust. He ordered champagne to be sent up, of course, and the combined effect of the alcohol and the anticipation soon had Lynne in a state of wild euphoria. Before long she had Jonathan stripped of his clothes and, kneeling before him, paid homage to his sturdy erection.

'Oh, what a lovely strong prick!' she exclaimed, flicking her tongue across its bulging purplish head.

'Hey, take it easy!' he laughed, putting his hands in her armpits to lift her to her feet. 'We've got all night, remember!'

'Is one night long enough?' she wondered aloud, her mind befuddled.

Jonathan laughed indulgently. 'If not, you can take me home with you and we'll do it all over again. Now lie down, there's a good girl. I want to examine every last inch of you, so you're to lie there and let me, okay?'

It was pure bliss to feel him touch her all over with his fingers and lips, stroking and kissing her into a state of deliciously sensual laziness. By the time he came to nuzzle at her soft downy mound she was open and ready for him, sighing contentedly as his tongue slipped below her mons and found her expectant clitoris rising to meet it, the tiny plexus of nerves where her sensitivity was most concentrated. He touched her there so delicately that she held her breath, savouring the exquisite subtlety of the feelings that his ministrations were producing. A heat was radiating out from that spot to the rest of her body, keeping her desire on a slow fuse.

Lynne reached out and caressed his broad, muscular shoulders. He felt different from Nick, solid and meaty where her ex had been less well developed, and somehow that was like a metaphor of the difference between them. Jonathan seemed more dependable, had more substance to him.

He was also a tender and considerate lover, pleasuring her in ways that Nick would never have had time for. While his lips mouthed her nipple, his fingers played around the whole of her lower region, stroking her thighs and stomach as much as he caressed her vulva, eroticising the whole area. The yearning she felt for him grew rapidly and yet it was never intolerable. He let her have just as much as she craved, but no more. He was bringing her up to her peak of arousal in gradual stages, requiring no more of her than that she should lie there and enjoy it.

Soon Lynne's whole body was vibrant with controlled longing for him. She could have let herself come, propelled herself into a self-indulgent orgy of sensation, but that wasn't what she wanted. Her first orgasm with Jonathan had to be mutual, and she was prepared to wait for it. Once he was inside her, she guessed that neither of them would have to wait long.

At last he was kneeling between her thighs, his penis rearing impatiently as he parted her labia with careful fingers. 'Oh, you're so beautiful!' he sighed, looking down at the open-petalled rose of her vulva. Soon she could feel his glans just plugging her entrance and she embraced it firmly with her labia, letting him know that she wanted him to come in deeper. He took his time, inching in slowly so that she could feel the extent of him as he slipped into her, expanding her vaginal walls until they fitted snugly around him. Then, when he was docked in her up to the hilt, he uttered a low groan of relief.

'God, I've dreamed of this so often!' he sighed, kissing her breasts and then her lips as he lay still within her. 'And it's a million times better than I ever imagined.'

'Mm!' she answered contentedly, stroking his back. 'It feels so right, so natural to have you inside me. Oh Jonathan, I'd begun to despair of ever feeling like this again with a man.'

He started to move, almost imperceptibly, just a slight withdrawal each time followed by a small sinking back. Lynne could feel herself opening up and up, becoming increasingly wet and sensitive inside. She tilted her hips to let him penetrate her even more deeply, embracing the whole of him, shaft and tip, with slow contracting of her muscles, and the lovely gentle pre-orgasmic waves began to flow freely throughout her whole system, making her incandescent with contained energy.

'You're all lit up!' Jonathan told her, wonderingly, confirming the way she felt. 'Glowing all over, like a Halloween pumpkin!'

'You look wonderful, too,' she told him truthfully. His eyes were the bluest she'd ever seen them, and his skin radiated light.

It seemed impossible to keep going much longer without releasing all that pent-up pressure but somehow they kept on and on, in no hurry to squander all their riches on one frantic spending-spree. Lynne would never have believed she could control herself so completely, yet with Jonathan it was easy just to relish the moment, without needing more. She felt as if every cell in her body were on fire and the central furnace of her desire was still burning at a steady pace, feeding the heat by which she would eventually be consumed.

Then everything changed. Lynne began stroking Jonathan at the back of his neck and the stimulus finally triggered him into thrusting more rapidly. 'Oh God, Lynne!' he moaned, 'I'm going to come!' as the unstoppable rush began.

Lynne's reaction was swift and automatic. She clung to him, kissing his neck passionately while her sexual excitement accelerated in seconds, triggering one of the most intense climaxes she'd ever known. Her body convulsed over and over with the spreading waves that went far beyond their source to invade every corner of her, filling her with rapture. She felt floaty and light, giving herself up completely to the timeless cadence of her orgasm, effortlessly riding the waves until they were reduced to a mild fluttering, bringing her gently back. Then, instead of the sad nostalgia she'd become used to feeling with Nick, Lynne was filled with a warm and uplifting sense of security.

She lay musing for a while with her head against his chest, relishing the slowing of his breath to a soothing rise and fall. Every second that passed made her more sure of her feelings for him until she kissed the place where his heart was beating then said, quietly, 'Jonathan, I think I love you.'

He hugged her close. 'It's mutual. I've felt like this about you for quite a while.' He raised himself on one elbow and looked down at her, his face serious. 'Lynne, there's been no-one serious in my life for quite a while now. Not since I broke off an engagement, two years ago. I thought I could never learn to trust any woman again, let alone love one. But now I know I can.'

She reached up and kissed his lips. They were comfortingly warm and soft. 'I've got some debris to clear out of my life, as you know. But now I feel in a much stronger position to do it, thanks to you.'

'I'll help you, Lynne. Any way I can.'

Her heart sang at the thought that she was no longer alone, that she would have someone by her as she underwent the painful process of divorce and the re-building of her life. Only one small shadow remained, the one that had dogged her silently all day in Brighton. If she could just see her dad again, to know he was all right and still cared about her, everything in her life would be perfect.

Chapter Twelve

LYNNE WAS DISCONCERTED to find that the scene where Carol was seduced by Penny was to take up an entire episode of *Night Owls*.

'We think it will boost our ratings,' Don told her.

'And it will make a star of you overnight, my dear!' Blake added, with a wink.

'Are you sure you're ready for all the publicity?' Jonathan asked her later, when they had a moment together.

Lynne sighed. 'I suppose it can't be worse than what's happened already. And this time I'm sure it won't ruin my love-life. Thank God we're in the same business, Jon. I know you'll be understanding.'

He gave her a surreptitious kiss, then they went back on to the studio floor to prepare for their scene together. Since they had become close, Lynne found a special excitement in acting with Jonathan. Not that their interchange was particularly significant. They still only indulged in polite chat at the bar. But just to have him there on set, his blue eyes sending special messages that only she could decode, was a thrill in itself.

Sandra approached her at lunch time. 'I think we should have a chat, Lynne. Are you needed this afternoon?'

'Not until four-ish.'

'Okay. Shall we find a quiet place to talk?'

They ended up in an unused dressing-room. Lynne felt anxious, and she decided to come clean with Sandra straight away. 'Look, I'm still nervous about doing this. It's not going to be easy for me.'

'Me neither,' Sandra admitted. 'I've always managed to keep my private life quite separate from my public image. Now I'll be coming out with a vengeance, and I don't know what the consequences will be.'

Lynne was relieved to find the actress was sympathetic. For the first time it occurred to her that Sandra might be taking more of a risk than herself in playing a lesbian on television.

They went on to discuss how Carol was going to react to Penny's advances.

'Okay, let me summarise,' Lynne said at last. 'Carol responds at first out of curiosity.'

'And loneliness,' Sandra reminded her.

'Yes. And she definitely gets off on it. But afterwards she has second thoughts because she's worried about being pigeon-holed.'

'Okay. That bit where she says she never had any sexual feelings towards women before is significant, I think. It shows it's not the real thing.'

'Fine. I'm happy with that, if you are.'

'I told Don I'd like us to deal with the issue more seriously in later episodes. He's promised to let Penny do some soul-searching, then she'll go along to a lesbian club and things will develop from there.

He sees it as a natural extension to the Night Owls scene, so it should work well. Ultimately, though, I'd like to see her in a stable relationship with another woman.'

'I don't know what's in store for Carol,' Lynne sighed. 'Frankly, I feel quite vulnerable.'

It was the truth. She suspected that Carol could easily be written out once she'd turned Penny down.

'Don't worry,' Sandra smiled, giving her a hug. 'I'm sure they think you're an asset to the show. The bar wouldn't be the same without you.'

But I don't want to spend the rest of my soap life stuck behind a bar, Lynne thought sourly. Perhaps her scene with Sandra was her one big chance to show what she could do.

On the morning when they were due to shoot the crucial scene, Lynne was delighted to receive a bouquet with a 'Good Luck' card from Jonathan. He wasn't needed that day, but in a way Lynne was glad. She could do without the distraction of his very heterosexual presence.

Instead, she tried to get into the right mood to fancy Sandra. It wasn't too difficult. The actress was very pretty in a pixie-ish way, with ash-blonde hair cut short with a feathered fringe emphasising her clear grey eyes, and a slim, boyish figure. They cleared the set except for the technicians and Chris, the director, urged them to take their time. The preliminary scene, where Penny invited Carol back to her flat, had been shot the week before and now they had all day to perfect the love scene.

The action took place on the couch in Penny's sitting-room, with k d lang singing softly in the background. The situation was reminiscent of

Lynne's experience with Zoe, which made it both easier and harder. They began by discussing men.

'You don't have a boyfriend, do you Carol?'

Remembering how she'd felt when Nick had betrayed her, it wasn't hard to say Carol's next line with conviction. 'No, and I don't want one right now. I've had enough of men!'

'I don't blame you. Most men haven't a clue how to treat a woman, especially in bed.' Sandra put out her hand and caressed Lynne's hair. Her voice became low and seductive. 'Have you ever had a woman make love to you?'

'No.'

'Maybe you've fantasised about it. Most of us have.'

'Maybe . . .'

Sandra smiled. 'Tell me about it,' she invited, softly.

'What, my lesbian fantasy?' Sandra nodded, stroking her cheek. 'Well, it starts with me going to a club and getting picked up by a woman. I mean, I don't know – at first, I just think she's being friendly. Anyway, she invites me back to her flat . . . Oh!'

'What's the matter, Carol?'

Lynne managed to summon up a blush. 'Well, I didn't want you to think . . . I mean, it's a bit like us now, isn't it?'

'But we know each other already, don't we? I wanted to see you because I'm sorry for the way I acted before, over Andrew.That's the trouble with men. They make you act in despicable ways. Anyway, let's forget all that now. Go on, tell me more about your fantasy.'

Lynne was finding Sandra's touch very arousing,

and guessed that her embarrassment at being in front of the cameras was making her portrayal of Carol all the more realistic.

'We're sitting on the sofa and she starts to tell me how attractive I am, and stuff like that.'

'Well, you are, Carol. I think you're lovely too.'

'Then she puts her arm around . . .'

'Like this?'

'Sandra drew her close, staring straight into her eyes. Lynne took a deep breath. She knew the next move, but it was still a bit of a shock to think she was about to perform for millions of viewers. She put that out of her mind and tried to think herself back into the character of Carol. 'Yes,' she breathed. 'Just like this. And then she kisses me.'

They had rehearsed their first screen kiss a couple of times, but now Sandra was putting far more feeling into it. As their tongues entwined Lynne felt a rush of excitement through her veins and when Sandra's hand crept gently under her T-shirt and began caressing her breast she began to get quite carried away.

For a moment, their lips parted and Sandra whispered, 'Is this like your fantasy, Carol?'

Soon they were both horizontal on the sofa and kissing passionately. There was dead silence on the studio floor. Although the moves had been carefully worked out in advance, Lynne felt it was happening for the first time. She shivered with anticipation as her bra was undone, exposing her breasts to inquisitive fingers, and gasped as Sandra's mouth found one of her thrusting nipples and sucked it to a rosy peak.

'Oh, Penny!' she murmured, stroking the other woman's small breasts in return.

Soon they were both stripped to their panties, which was considered to be as far as they could go even on late-night television. When Penny put her hand down the front of Carol's panties there came the cry of 'Cut!' and Lynne had to make an effort to shake herself out of the scene and back into the reality of being in Studio B, with half a dozen men standing by. Chris came bustling up. 'That was great, girls! Well done, both of you.'

Then came the hard part. Lynne had to strip off completely so they could take a shot of her and Sandra going into the bedroom. Fortunately it was from the rear, but they had to repeat the action three times before Chris was happy with it.

After that the pair had to snuggle down beneath the duvet in Penny's bedroom. They'd already shot several scenes between Penny and Andrew on this same set, so the irony would no doubt be appreciated by their regular viewers. Just for a moment Lynne reflected on what she was doing. Here she was totally nude in bed with another woman, on prime-time TV. If someone had told her six months ago that she'd be doing that she'd have laughed in their face!

Then the call came. 'Shot twenty-two, and . . . action!'

There was to be more passionate kissing and fondling of each other above the waist. The duvet kept rucking up, hiding their breasts, so they had to have it pinned down in place.

'They want everyone to see our beautiful breasts!' Sandra whispered, with a grimace. 'God knows what Cheryl is going to make of all this!' Lynne knew she was referring to her partner. Jonathan had told her they'd been living together for three years.

After a few more shots of Penny kissing Carol's breasts came the sequence Lynne was dreading most of all. Penny would be seen disappearing beneath the duvet and then the camera would remain on Carol's face for a full twenty seconds, monitoring her reactions. As the music of k d lang swelled to a crescendo, Lynne had to feign heightening pleasure and then fake an orgasm. It was not going to be easy.

For one thing she was afraid that Sandra would actually perform cunnilingus on her while out of sight. She'd said she wouldn't, but what if she changed her mind and decided to make the whole thing more realistic? Already Lynne could feel the other woman getting into position with her head between her thighs, her hot breath fanning her vulva. She was excited, but if she was to remain in control of her facial expressions it was no good getting too worked up. She had to make it last for exactly twenty seconds, not a moment more or less.

So when the call came to start shooting, Lynne began silently counting. 'One thousand, two thousand, three thousand . . .' As the count went on she began to writhe and moan, but although she could feel Sandra's hair brushing against her thighs her head remained mercifully still. At 'fifteen thousand' she decided to have her orgasm and threw her head back, giving a long loud moan and muttering 'Oh God!' with ever-increasing fervour. The relief when she heard the word 'Cut!' was enormous, but then she began praying that she wouldn't have to go through it all again.

'That's fine!' she heard Chris say.

Sandra's head popped up, giggling. 'Well done! It was suffocating down there!'

They positioned themselves for the last shot of the day, lying in each other's arms. But while Penny was rambling on about how much she'd enjoyed their love-making, Carol had to look doubtful. The scene ended with her gazing at a photo of Andrew that Penny had forgotten to remove from her dressing-table. 'How appropriate!' Lynne thought.

By the end of the day, Lynne felt utterly drained. The one thing she didn't need was a letter on her mat from her solicitor, but that was what she got. The date for the divorce hearing was now set. She and Nick had decided to say nothing to their solicitors about their abortive attempt at a reunion. That way the proceedings could go forward smoothly.

It was growing cold now that the evening was closing in, so she decided to light a wood fire in the grate. As she applied a match to the kindling, Lynne felt very low. Life seemed flat again, now that her big scene was in the can, and she was depressed about the divorce. She rang Jonathan and asked him to come over, needing his company badly. He was with her inside an hour, bringing a take-away pizza with him.

As they sat on the sofa eating out of the box and drinking beer from cans, she admitted that she felt worried about her future.

'I don't know how much longer I've got in *Night Owls*, Jon. I can't help remembering how Hazel was kicked out and I was brought in more or less overnight. They could easily do the same thing to me.'

'They could, but I doubt they will. Not for a good while, anyway. They like to establish continuity with their characters, Lynne. I'm willing to bet that if Hazel hadn't developed a drinking problem they'd have kept her on a lot longer.'

'And then there's us,' Lynne continued tentatively.

'What about us? We're doing fine, aren't we?'

'Yes, but this divorce has brought it all home. I mean, I thought Nick and I were meant for each other too, but look how that's turned out.'

'Have you always been this insecure?'

'Insecure?' Lynne reflected. 'I suppose I am. But what happened with Nick didn't help.'

'Neither did what happened with your father, I imagine.'

'Yes, that was terrible! One minute he was there and everything was normal, the next minute he was gone and my world was turned upside down.'

'Hardly surprising then. You must hate him.'

'Oh no! I don't hate him!'

'Don't you? I would. Or I might hate my mother instead. Is that what happened, Lynne?'

'I don't know.'

'Have you ever truly explored how you felt, I wonder? Or is it all buried inside, festering away?'

Lynne shrugged. 'I didn't have any counselling or anything, if that's what you mean.'

'Or a friend or relative to talk to?'

'No, I didn't mention it to anyone. I was too ashamed. I was really pissed off when they found out at school through a friend of Mum's, but I was leaving at the end of that year so I didn't worry too much about it.'

Jonathan looked thoughtful. Then he said, 'Lynne, sit over there for a minute.'

'What? Why?'

'You'll see. I just want to put some distance

between us.' Frowning, she did as he asked, sitting down in the armchair opposite. 'Right. Now pretend I'm your dad. What have you got to say to me?'

'Hey, wait a minute! I don't want to talk about this.'

'I don't mean talk *about* your father. I'm asking you to talk *to* him. Just imagine I'm him, and I've walked back through that door and into your life again. What would you say to me?'

'I'd probably say . . . oh, this is impossible!'

'Try.'

Lynne began in a flippant tone. 'Okay. Hi, Dad. I never expected to see you again. So why did you walk out on us?'

'Why do *you* think I did?'

'Well, I thought lots about it, obviously. I knew you and Mum didn't get on, you were always rowing. I used to lie in bed listening, and sometimes I'd creep out on to the landing so I could hear better.'

'We wanted to keep you out of it, Lynne.'

'Well, it didn't work. I was even more upset because I didn't know exactly what was going on. And when you left I was devastated.'

'What did your mother say about my leaving?'

'Not a lot. I remember asking her if there was anyone else. She said she couldn't say. I never knew if there *was* someone – but she couldn't talk about it – or if she didn't know.'

'How did your life change after I'd gone?'

'My school work suffered. I only passed three of my exams. And I distanced myself from my friends. I was so afraid they'd find out what had happened at home.'

'But you had a boyfriend?'

'Yes. I met Nick after I'd moved out into a bedsit. We married the day after my eighteenth birthday. I suppose I was looking for the security I'd lost.'

'So it was my fault, was it, that your marriage failed?'

'Maybe.'

'Then you must be very angry with me.'

'Yes. Yes, I am!' Lynne felt the old hurt returning, the bitter taste of her disillusion resurfacing. 'For months and months I waited to hear from you. I told myself that it was Mum you'd walked out on, not me. Every time the phone rang or a letter fell on to the mat I'd tell myself, 'It's him!' but it never was. That's what I can't forgive you for, abandoning me along with Mum.'

'So what would you like to do to me, Lynne?'

'I'd like to punch your face!'

'Okay, go on then.' Jonathan held a cushion up in front of his face and Lynne aimed a hefty blow at it. 'And again, Lynne! One for every time you woke in the night and remembered I wasn't there!'

'I'd punch myself silly!'

'Then do it!'

Lynne delivered a battery of blows to the plump cushion, wondering how long it could hold out against her fury. She continued until she was puffing and panting, and each time she stopped Jonathan encouraged her to continue. 'Now one for every time that phone rang and it wasn't me!'

Eventually, feeling utterly exhausted by the physical expression of her wrath, Lynne collapsed on the floor weeping. It was good to cry. She hadn't done it for a long time.

She felt Jonathan's arms around her. 'That's

good,' he murmured. 'Let it out.'

When her tears had subsided, Lynne went to fetch some kitchen roll. Jonathan followed, and put the kettle on. They sat down on stools, facing each other, and Lynne was reminded of when Jenny had turned up and the three of them had confronted each other for the first time.

'I don't know what that was all about,' she told him, shaking her head. 'It seemed to come out of nowhere. But I do feel much better for it, I must say.'

'What we did is called "psychodrama", Lynne. I haven't told you this before, but it's what I've been training to do for the past two years.'

'What? You've been using me as a guinea pig, to practise on?'

'No, honestly, that's not how it was. It just occurred to me that you could do with facing up to your feelings about your father, and that's the best way I know.'

She smiled wryly. 'Well, it seems to work, doesn't it?'

He got up and made them some tea. Lynne wanted to know more. 'So you get people to act out their feelings about other people, do you?'

'That's about it. Usually it takes a few sessions before we start to make progress. I began by doing it myself, so I know the value of this method.'

'Do you think it could help me some more?'

'Probably. In any case, if you want me to help you find your father I'd recommend doing some more work on your feelings about him first.'

'You're serious about this, aren't you?'

Jonathan came towards her, his blue eyes alight. 'I love you, Lynne, and I'd do anything to make you happy. I know you've had a rough time, and I want to make it up to you. I'll stand by you through the divorce and then, if it's what you want, we can build a future together.'

Lynne felt a lump rise in her throat. Not even in the early days with Nick had she felt this loved, this supported. She reached out and clung to him, her eyes filling with tears once more.

'I tried acting scenes with Nick,' she told him, as they drank their tea. 'You know, rôle-playing games. "Me Tarzan, you Jane" kind of stuff. He found it a turn-on.'

'Did you?'

'Kind of, for a while. Then I realised I was being used in some kind of a power struggle.'

'In psychodrama we play it for real, Lynne. And the results speak for themselves.'

She took his hand. 'That's what I like about you, Jonathan. You're completely straight with me. No games-playing, no subterfuge.'

'You're making me sound boring!'

'Not at all. I feel good knowing that when we make love it's me you're thinking of, not another woman or some fantasy figure. With Nick, I was never sure.'

He took her in his arms and kissed her, gently at first and then with increasing passion as something ignited in both of them. They went into the front room, where the fire was still sending out its comforting glow. Nick lit the candles on the mantelpiece and turned out the main light, plunging the room into mysterious shadow. Lynne put some quiet music on then stretched out luxuriously like a cat in front of the fire. She ached all over for his touch, and the reassuring feeling of being joined to him at some fundamental level.

Slowly he stripped her, warming up each new area of exposed skin with his lips and hands before removing another garment. Lynne lay passively, watching him. His face was so concentrated on her body, the blue of his eyes darkly aglow with reflected light. She reached up and felt his tousled hair, soft and sleek beneath her fingers. Every part of him was precious to her. Was this what love had been like the first time around? Somehow she didn't think so.

When only her panties remained, Jonathan began to remove his own clothes. They hugged each other close on the thick rug, basking in the warmth of the fire, and Lynne felt the warmth within growing too. She wanted him, but they had all the time in the world. He had taught her to take it slowly, to enjoy every moment for its own sake without forever striving onward. It was like travelling by bike down a winding country lane instead of taking a fast car on the motorway, and the sounds, sights and scents were so much more wonderful when experienced at a leisurely pace.

Once Jonathan was lying there naked, his penis half erect, Lynne decided she wanted to take the initiative for a while. She planted soft kisses all over his chest, enjoying his shuddering response when she pulled at his tiny nipples with her lips. Her hands roved over his flat stomach and down his thighs, feeling the muscles tighten beneath his flesh. She moved her mouth slowly down his left side, accompanied by agonised protests.

'Lynne! If you knew what you're doing to me! Oh God, that's exquisitely tormenting!'

She felt him shudder again, his hips writhing, and brushed the flat of her hand briefly over the curly bush where his penis was lying, already more solid than before. Then she reached down and touched the soft sac that held his testicles, caressing it with tender strokes until he was moaning almost continually. One finger slipped down behind, to find the crevice between his buttocks and probe a little. Then she bent her head to lick the very tip of his glans, and his groans redoubled.

'Oh, Lynne! You can do that as much as you like!'

She'd never enjoyed pleasuring a man so much. With Nick her fellatio had always been a somewhat brief preliminary to the main action, but now it was different. Jonathan burned with a slower flame, which she delighted in slowly feeding until it was a smouldering inferno. Taking his shaft delicately between her fingers she rubbed the underside a little and soon the flesh was firming up, pushing the purplish glans out of its protective covering until she could see the whole of its shiny surface.

Lynne pressed her tongue into the slit and tasted the first of his secretions. She put the tip between her lips. The shaft made a thrusting movement and soon her mouth was halfway down it while she continued to fondle his balls, pressing her body close to his so that her breasts were pushed against his right thigh. She opened her legs and got astride his shin, finding his hard kneecap very stimulating to the softly opened tissues of her vulva. Now she was completely wrapped around his leg, like some dryad around a tree, and her mouth continued to lick and suck at his full-grown organ, making him ready for her and her for him.

'Turn around, let me lick you!' she heard him say at last.

Obediently she reversed her position and, as her

lips closed over his glans again, she felt his tongue probe between her labia and find the erect little button nestling within. Lynne sighed with delight, relaxing as he tongued her up and down, lingering first at the liquid entrance to her sex and then moving to her impatient clitoris. She felt that her consciousness was split between her sensual organs and his, blurring the boundaries between them and making the experience truly mutual.

His hands began stroking her buttocks, and she felt their smoothness through the medium of his palms. She reached down the hairy planes of his thighs, and knew that her touch was awakening him to the feel of his own skin. They were both engaged in an act of revelation, each helping the other to discover their physical selves anew, and delighting in the joint exploration.

'I want to come into you,' she heard him murmur, his voice tense with desire. 'Are you ready for me?'

In answer she guided his finger to her vulva and let him feel her wetness. His penis gave a surge and she went to sit astride him on the rug but he held her back.

'No, let's get into that chair,' he suggested.

He was looking at her rocking chair. The doweling that joined the arms to the seat had wide gaps in between. Lynne took up her position on the cushion with her thighs spread apart while Jonathan clambered on with his legs between the wooden dowels and his feet on the floor. Then he slowly eased himself into her.

It was blissfully relaxing to rock to and fro with him inside her, letting the momentum of the chair do most of the work. While she floated lazily up and down Jonathan paid full attention to her breasts, lifting the weighty globes to his mouth and licking at her pert nipples until she felt a heady voluptuousness take hold of her. She wallowed in the pure sensuality, almost unaware of her impending climax until she recognised that the slow throbbing in her vulva had turned to a more urgent shuddering within and she threw her head back, uttering a little cry of surprise as the first of the ecstatic spasms pervaded her body.

'Oh, that was fantastic!' she sighed. 'I wasn't expecting it right then.'

'Good. I love surprising you.'

He lifted up her hair and planted a delicate kiss on the nape of her neck, making her shiver. His hands squeezed at her breasts, thumbs pressing on her still quivering nipples. They kissed mouth to mouth, keeping perfectly still, and then Lynne began just tightening a little on his penis, to make sure he maintained his erection. He was making tiny movements inside her, as if his organ were twisting against her walls. She giggled: it was like being tickled internally.

Jonathan put his hands beneath her and cupped her buttocks as he increased the pace. She was rising up and down, riding on his hands now. This time she wanted to make him come too. Already her clitoris had kicked back into pulsating life and she was clutching at his erection with her vaginal walls, willing him to join her in the ultimate consummation. Yet although she could feel herself moving inexorably towards a second climax he held back, and she met the fierce oncoming wave of her orgasm on her own. It buffeted her senses, making her only half aware of his soft nibbling at her nipples and his thumbs reaching between her buttocks. She groaned with the sheer power of it, feeling it assault her back and front, knowing no barrier. The hot reverberations continued until she was sated and sank back against the chair, her limbs exhausted and her chest covered with a light dewy film.

'I wanted you to come too that time,' she complained softly.

'I prefer to wait. I love watching you come, Lynne. I've never seen any sight so beautiful.'

His words evoked a few last shudders from her, fading echoes of her desire. Again they kissed, and this time her lips felt swollen almost to insensitivity she was so thoroughly spent. For a while Jonathan cradled her as they rocked softly, as if in time to inaudible music, for the music that Lynne had put on earlier had long ceased. Only the sound of their breathing, the faint beat of their hearts and the intermittent crackling of the fire were witness to their passion.

They changed over so that Lynne was astride him, and she rode up and down on his long, thick shaft as the chair continued to swing to their rhythm. This time the friction against her clitoris was even more impossible to resist and she came within a few minutes, gasping as the sweetness overtook her again with a juddering intensity that sent shock after shock of fiery energy through her. Looking down through bleary eyes she saw Jonathan was gazing up at her, smiling, his face alight with love.

They embraced and Lynne collapsed with her head against his chest while he stroked her hair. She was amazed to find a lover who wasn't triggered off by her own orgasming. They continued to rock back and forth to the gentle lullaby of their heartbeat while the fire was reduced to glowing embers. Then he began to stroke her breasts and her longing for him returned. This time she dearly wanted them to meet in a timeless climax, to feel the simultaneous pulse of their mutual pleasure.

She lowered herself on to his slightly waning erection and soon it hardened within her so she quickened the pace, wanting to arouse him further.

'Take it easy,' Jonathan drawled. 'We've still got half the night.'

'I want you to come inside me,' she murmured into his ear.

'I am inside you.'

She giggled. 'You know exactly what I mean!'

'What's the hurry?'

'Hurry? My God, I've already come three times! Now I want you to join me.'

'I don't have to, you know. I could keep this up all night.'

She gave him a kiss. 'I know, darling, but just as you like to watch me maybe I like to watch you. So please, will you indulge me?'

'Oh, all right. But we'll have to get back on the mat.'

He laid her down gently, and then plunged into her. This time she was left in no doubt about his intent. Each deep, powerful stroke was calculated to bring them both to a fever pitch of desire and as Lynne felt herself approaching the crest once again she knew that this time he would join her in a climax of overwhelming force. She was almost afraid as she was swept along, feeling him hard and strong, knowing that her previous solo performances would pale in significance beside what was about to happen.

It began as a light, exhilarating rapture but quickly deepened into a synchronised pulse that plunged them both into a vortex of feeling and emotion, a point where flesh merged and identity vanished while they plunged into a timeless void of pure sensation. Dimly Lynne was aware of his penis still penetrating her, but it was as if he had used it to bore straight through to her heart. Long after the beauty of it had resolved itself into mere memory Lynne clung to the man who had shown her what love could be like when it was truly shared. Words failed her, even kisses and embraces felt inadequate. She could only lie there in his arms and wonder.

They fell asleep before the dying fire, and when Lynne awoke the coals were out, the candles spluttering and she felt cold. Carefully she disentangled her body from his and got to her feet while he slept on. She sat in the rocking chair for a while, looking down on him, and knew that although they might equal the love they had made that night they would never surpass it. Whatever happened between them in future they had, for this one night at least, possessed each other entirely. And, for the moment, she was perfectly content with that.

Studio B was buzzing with the success of 'that scene'. There had been calls of protest to Sphere TV, which meant that the ratings would certainly be up when they repeated the episode on Sunday night's omnibus edition. Don had met Lynne in the foyer with a beam on his face and told her that he wanted to see her and Jonathan, pronto!

Even so, Lynne felt very nervous as she followed Jonathan down the corridor.

'Don't worry,' he smiled, taking her hand. 'He wants to congratulate you, that's all.'

'But why does he want to see you as well? Surely it should be me and Sandra. I don't understand.'

'All will soon be revealed,' he grinned as the door marked 'Don Chisholm, Producer' loomed into view.

'Take a seat, both of you.' Don threw Lynne a smile as she sank into a chair. 'Congratulations, Lynne. I knew you'd pull it off. And I know what courage it took to give it a go. The question is, where do we go from here?' The door opened and Rob Bates walked in. 'Ah, hello Rob. Are you ready to explain the future to these two?'

'Sure.' He put his folder down on the desk and surveyed them both. 'First, I want to say I think you did a really good job, Lynne . . .'

'We've already been through all that,' Don said brusquely. 'Can we move on? Lynne's sure to be wondering what's going to happen to Carol.'

'Of course. Well, Lynne, you'll be glad to know that we've a new romance for you. It will take a few weeks to develop, of course, but as it's with someone you already know the viewers shouldn't be too surprised.'

Lynne and Jonathan looked at each other, then burst out laughing.

'I think they've guessed!' she heard Don say.

'Won't Penny be mad with Andrew!' Jonathan grinned.

'On both counts, probably,' Rob pointed out. 'She won't know which of you she's most jealous of. Neat, huh?'

'But is it going to last?' Lynne asked him. 'I mean, will you give us a happy ending?'

Rob and Don exchanged glances. 'Now you know I can't answer that,' Rob hedged. 'But I think the chances are good. That's as far as I'm prepared to go.'

'*Night Owls* isn't so different from life, you know,' Don added. 'There are never any guarantees. And you won't know what's going to happen until it's written into the script. Even then there are last minute changes.'

'Well as long as we get some steamy love scenes that's good enough for me,' Jonathan smiled, winking at Lynne.

'Me too,' she said, giggling. The thought had just crossed her mind that if Carol and Andrew made love anything like Lynne and Jonathan, then the ratings would soar sky high!